Aliens, Drywall, and a Unicycle

"For me, the most beautiful books are always
the strange ones, and *Aliens, Drywall, and a Unicycle* is both
strange and beautiful. It's a novel about a culture—the 90s—
that, in this moment, we're both leaving behind and reviving.
Like so many of the great lean works of fiction—*Cannery Row,
Jesus' Son*—Kevin St. Jarre's book obeys its own singular vision
of place, character, idea and, more than anything, meaning.
And, like all the best books of its kind, this novel trembles
on the verge of almost making no sense—and yet, by the
final pages, I found myself feeling that rare emotion
that only truly unique art inspires."
—**Jaed Coffin**, author of *A Chant to Soothe Wild Elephants*
and *Roughhouse Friday*

"*Aliens, Drywall, and a Unicycle*—the title doesn't
even begin to get to all the juxtapositional hijinks in this
poignant, funny, and breakneck debut. Our man Tom lives in
an apartment building with a cast of alternately alluring, zany,
dangerous, and lovable characters whose stories ineluctably
become his own. Kevin St. Jarre writes with life and humor
and blessed heartfelt economy, reaches into souls and pulls out
secrets it turns out we all share. Antic, compassionate, sweet
and sometimes deadly, this novel will keep you reading till the
batteries run out in your flashlight, dark night of the soul."
—**Bill Roorbach**, author of *Life Among Giants,
The Remedy for Love*, and *The Girl of the Lake*

Aliens, Drywall, and a Unicycle Copyright © 2020 Kevin St. Jarre

Paperback ISBN 13: 978-1-64599-067-3
E-book ISBN 13: 978-1-64599-068-0
Kindle ISBN 13: 978-1-64599-069-7

LCCN: 2020942759

Publisher's Cataloging-In-Publication Data:
(Prepared by The Donohue Group, Inc.)

Names: St. Jarre, Kevin, author.
Title: Aliens, Drywall, and a Unicycle / Kevin St. Jarre.
Description: Farmington, Maine U.S.A. : Encircle Publications, LLC, [2020]
Identifiers: ISBN 9781645990673 (paperback) | ISBN 9781645990680
(ebook) | ISBN 9781645990697 (Kindle)
Subjects: LCSH: Neighbors—New Hampshire—Fiction. |
Self-perception—Fiction. | Meaning (Philosophy)—Fiction. | Life
change events—Fiction. | Apartment houses—New Hampshire—Fiction.
Classification: LCC PS3619.T2467 A45 2020 (print) | LCC PS3619.T2467
(ebook) | DDC 813/.6--dc23

Editor: Cynthia Brackett-Vincent
Interior layout and cover design by Deirdre Wait, High Pines Creative, Inc.
Cover images © Getty Images

Published by: Encircle Publications, LLC
P.O. Box 187
Farmington, ME 04938

Visit: http://encirclepub.com

Sign up for Encircle Publications newsletter and specials
http://eepurl.com/cs8taP

Printed in U.S.A.

Aliens, Drywall, and a Unicycle

KEVIN ST. JARRE

Encircle Publications, LLC
Farmington, Maine U.S.A.

*For my daughter and her
generation of lovable zombies.
I'm proud of you, Laura, and I love you.*

1

Unpacking is infinitely better than packing. When a person tries to fit his old life into boxes, it's an ongoing series of decisions about what gets abandoned and what does not.

Tom Tibbetts was unpacking. Bits of his old life appeared from the containers, settled into the corners of his new life, and filled the cramped apartment. The place smelled of fresh but cheap paint, new but bargain carpet, and Pine-Sol. The walls and the ceiling were white, and the same beige carpet ran through every room in the place. Tom had the interior door open, and a breeze coming in through the screen door did its best to push the smell of chemicals out the windows.

His life had imploded, leaving him hurt and cynical. The entire thing was quite complicated, he believed, and no one seemed to really understand. Eventually, he began to see everyone as either hostile, stupid, or some combination. He knew he wasn't likeable; he knew people couldn't sympathize. Remembering his father's saying, "If you meet more than two assholes in the same day, it's actually you who is the asshole," he understood where he stood. He just couldn't see the way back up.

He had taken a job in a college town after the students had returned for the fall semester, and they had snapped up the better housing. Finding an apartment in the Cooper building, Tom was surrounded by neighbors. He was in apartment 2B in a three-story complex with nine units. His was the least desirable in the building, with neighbors above and below him, and on either side. Across the face of the building, at each floor, was a shared concrete balcony with a wrought-iron railing and stairs, and his door opened onto this. There was no interior stairwell.

Down on the street, someone Tom couldn't see shouted, "Hey! Fuck you, douchebag!"

It was quite a change from his previous address, where he'd had a house with a yard, a stockade fence, and a trail down to a brook. The house had come with Vicky, and it had stayed with her. What he missed most was his old dog, Wallace. More than a few times, especially after one of the many nasty fights with Vicky, Tom had thought the dog was the only friend he had in the world.

Wallace had loved to chase a ball, and they'd spent many hours in the dog park, just the two of them. Over the years, Wallace had slowed, turned grey, and Tom had known the inevitable was coming. The day Wallace died, he and Vicky held each other, crying, but when the next fight with Vicky came, Tom realized how alone he really was. It wasn't long after that day that Vicky gave him enough reason to leave.

In Portage, he had his new apartment, with no dog, and no girlfriend. He'd brought along two houseplants, but they didn't add any sort of comfort. Instead, at best, they seemed like fellow refugees, and at worst, hostages.

However, he was not alone for long, and met his first neighbor before he was completely unpacked. She appeared at his doorway wearing cutoff jeans and a long-sleeve black shirt, bearing the oft-seen photo of Kurt Cobain in the cardigan he wore for the MTV Unplugged gig. Pushing Kurt out of shape were two obviously unrestrained breasts. Her dark hair was long and curly, and her feet were bare. She wore heavy eyeliner but no other make-up.

"Hey," she said through the screen.

"Hey."

"You need anything, I'm on top of you," she said.

Tom said nothing, but then she pointed upward and said, "I'm in the apartment above you."

"Cute," Tom said, wondering how many times she'd rehearsed that, or used it on previous tenants. She grinned, and he smiled in spite of himself.

"What's your name?" she asked.

"What's yours?" Tom asked.

"Brynn," she said.

"Brynn what?"

"Just Brynn," she said.

"No last name?"

She grinned again, and then asked, "So, she threw you out?"

"Who?" Tom asked, but he knew who. Vicky hadn't so much as thrown him out as she had replaced him. Throughout her life, Tom knew, Vicky was always on the lookout for the next upgrade, but she was never single between men. Her relationships tended to overlap. Of course, a guy doesn't believe he'll be another one of those stories, or layers, until after it happens to him.

"Whoever got you that sweater," she said.

It was a lime green v-neck, and Tom wasn't sure why it'd made the cut, even though it was his mother who'd given it to him years before.

"You want it?" he asked.

She giggled and leaned forward until first her breasts and then her forehead rested against the screen.

"You coming in?" he asked. "Or are you going to keep talking to me through the door?"

"I don't know you well enough yet," she said.

Looking her over, he knew there was no chance that she was as uncomplicated as she was trying to seem. Tom asked, "How old are you, Brynn?"

"Rude," she said, but then, "I'm twenty-three. How old are you?"

"I'm almost twenty years older than you," he said.

"I wasn't looking to hook up or anything," she said.

He said, "I wasn't implying that."

"You were checking me out a minute ago," she said.

"Was I?" he asked.

She said, "It's okay, men do that, but I wasn't looking to hook up. I've got a boyfriend."

He asked, "Is he a Nirvana fan, too?"

"A what?" she asked.

"The shirt," he said.

She looked down at her chest. "Oh right, I'm not really a fan of the music."

"Why the shirt then?" he asked, unable to help himself.

"I thought he went out really cool," she said.

Tom stopped unpacking, and said, "He was desperately depressed, chronically sick and in constant pain, addicted to heroin, and he blew his head off."

"*If* you believe he killed himself, which I do—I'm not one of those 'Courtney-killed-him-whackos'—but he had the courage to go through with it, and now he'll live always, forever young and beautiful," she said.

"Abandoning his daughter," he said.

"Abandoning his *millionaire* daughter."

"I bet she'd trade those millions for more time with her dad," he said.

She paused, tilted her head, and then said, "Whatever. You a teacher or something?"

"What makes you think I'm a teacher?" he asked.

"Well, you don't look like you lift heavy shit for a living," she said.

"A reporter. I'm taking a job at the newspaper," he said. "And I'm a writer."

"Isn't a newspaper reporter a writer?"

"I also write books," he said.

"Heh. For Kindle and stuff?" she asked.

"For Kindle and stuff," he said.

"Cool. I read a lot," she said.

"You do?"

"Don't seem so surprised. Eyeliner and tits don't make you stupid, you know," she said.

She was beginning to ruin his good mood. He said, "Listen, I didn't mean anything by it. I'm just moving in, unpacking... busy."

"I get it," she said. "I'll let you get to it. But you did think about hooking up with me." She grinned again, and then was gone from his doorway.

Tom blinked, stood there quietly for a moment, and wondered if all his neighbors were like Brynn.

Opening the next box, he pulled out four glasses, all different sizes. A small one he'd probably never use, a medium-sized plastic tumbler he would use to hold pens and pencils, a heavy pint glass, and a wine glass. Holding this last one, he looked around at the mess, abandoned the current box for another, and pulled out a bottle of Barolo and a corkscrew. He took the freshly poured glass out onto the balcony, leaned on the railing, and took a sip. The wine was warm and tannic, and the breeze smelled of asphalt. With the railing rocking on loose screws, Tom surveyed the view.

Portage, New Hampshire, had been a mill town, but when the mill went silent, the town reinvented itself as a college town. The local school, once Portage State College, had grown to the point of joining the university system, and had been reborn as Portage State University. It was hardly the same place. Once a town with sidewalks full of men carrying lunchboxes, and then a Main Street of shuttered shops through the tough years, Portage had become a town of young people, university events, yoga, coffee shops, and wandering grad students who never seemed to leave. From Tom's vantage point, he could see red brick, white vinyl siding, glass, pedestrians, small patches of green, and cars driving the short circuitous route that was the downtown. The entire vista sloped down to the river.

He looked forward to becoming a part of the community. Tom had been a reporter at a smaller newspaper, writing stories and occasionally contributing columns, until accepting the new position here at *The Portage Herald*.

"Are you a teacher or something?"

Tom turned and saw a man in his thirties, khaki shorts, and a loose button-down, short-sleeve shirt, Birkenstocks, with a shaggy head of hair.

"Why a teacher?" Tom asked. Did he really look *that* much like a teacher?

"It's the middle of a summer workday, and you're already drinking wine," he said, and smiled.

"Not a teacher," Tom said.

"I'm Ben, 2C," he said, thumbing back at his door.

"I'm Tom," he said and took another sip.

"Moving in?" Ben asked.

"Just about done. Just have to unpack the boxes," Tom said.

"What brought you here?" Ben asked.

Tom knew he'd be an object of curiosity for his new neighbors, but he thought it would look more like furtive glances and silent wondering. These people just walked up and started asking questions, as if in a rush to piece together some satisfying one-paragraph biography on the new guy. He knew, that whatever he said or did in reply supplied a puzzle piece. If he answered honestly and sincerely, that would provide info. If he answered curtly or snidely, that would provide info. If he silently went back into his apartment, that would provide info. Tom was a journalist, and he liked providing information, but about *other* people. Still, he was in a decent mood. Why not be friendly?

Tom smiled, and said, "I'm taking a job at the *Portage Herald*. I've been with the *Insider*. Did you go to school here?"

"I didn't go to school at all; I work at McDonald's," Ben said, and then added, a bit too loudly, "Want fries with that?"

Just as Tom was about to wonder if any of the neighbors would be able to participate in an intelligent conversation, Ben said, "Nope. No college, I. I'm proud to say that I'm an autodidact."

Tom's eyebrows lifted; that was potentially interesting. "What have you taught yourself?" he asked.

Ben said, "Name it, man, I never stop learning. I can't get enough."

"You read a lot?"

Ben said, "Man, I read *all* the time. Whatever I can find. I also learn from the Internet, TV, and movies. I learn from people, too, man, 'cause even though I'm, like, fuckin' Chatty Cathy right now, I'm actually, like, an intense listener, you know? Like, I listen, man, I listen *hard*, and it sticks. I just get bored if I can't be in charge of what I'm learning, you know? Like, be in control of what's going into my head, you know?"

Tom's hopes were initially raised, but now he was becoming a bit more skeptical.

"Tell me one thing you've learned. Impress me," Tom said.

"I don't learn shit to impress people, man. It's impossible to impress people, man. Even when people *are* impressed, it's so fucking uncool to *be* impressed with anything that no one will admit it, you know?" Ben said.

Tom smiled, nodded, and took another sip. So, the guy heard the word "autodidactic" on Jeopardy or something, and he's throwing it around now as an excuse for not furthering his education.

Ben said, "Alright, man, OK. How about this? I can speak Spanish."

"So can the better-prepared half of Americans," Tom said.

"Okay, man, but last Christmas? I could barely order at Taco Bell. Now, I speak Spanish, man."

"You speak Spanish," Tom said.

"I speak *fluent* Spanish, man. I watch movies in Spanish now and understand pretty much all of it. I know Russian, too. I'm learning Latin now," Ben said.

Tom lowered his glass. "You know Russian?"

"I'm not bullshitting you, man."

"Why are you learning languages?" Tom asked.

"Because otherwise when I read translations, there is an intermediary between me and the author, man, and they can't help but change it. Not just because of linguistic issues either, it's all about ego, man," Ben said. "All these far out ideas, but we get them filtered through some loser's biases before we get to experience them for ourselves."

It did occur to Tom that this fast-food genius had just referred to translators as losers. "Why do you work at McDonald's?"

"Why *not* work at McDonald's?" Ben asked. "Because people look down on it? I'm not going to switch jobs because of what other people think. I'm good at my job, and the people are friendly."

"But the pay," Tom said.

"Man, why are you looking for problems in my life? I make the money I need, and I spend the rest of my time learning and experiencing shit. Yeah, man, I'm not a kid anymore, and I work at McDonald's, but I don't live in my mother's basement, and I don't make a living building weapons or lying to people," Ben said.

Tom hadn't felt he was being negative, and said, "Look, I didn't mean…"

"You *did* mean it, man, but it's no thing. It's normal. We've been conditioned to be in a perpetually dissatisfied state, man, and we help each other maintain it," Ben said.

"The basis of ambition," Tom said.

"You say 'ambition' like it's a good thing, man," Ben said and grinned, and they both laughed.

"Look, man, you know the special sauce on Big Macs?" Ben asked.

"Thousand Island dressing? What about it?"

"Dude, see, exactly! Why? Why are you trying to take the 'special' out of the sauce? That's a myth, man. It's *not* Thousand Island dressing. Chefs working for McDonald's came up with that recipe. In fact, it changed over the years, but not that long ago, the CEO ordered everyone to go back to the original recipe, and they had to find it, because it got deleted, so they did some intense detective work and tracked it down. If it were just Thousand Island, they could've just bought some at the supermarket."

"Okay, sorry," Tom said. "So, what about the special sauce?"

Ben took a breath, and seemed to relax again, "It's special because it was made for one thing, to be the *special* sauce on a *special* sandwich. McDonald's sells 550 million Big Macs every year in the United States alone, dude. Can you think of a more successful sauce than that?"

Tom said, "Ketchup."

Ben paused, and then burst out laughing. "Right on, man, right on."

"I should get back to unpacking," Tom said.

"Cool, cool," Ben said.

"Nice meeting you," Tom said.

"You, too, Tom. I'll see you on the balcony," he said.

Tom went back into his apartment, drank the last of the glass of wine, and surveyed the work he had left to do.

2

The first Saturday in his new place, Tom woke, made some coffee, and turned on the TV. He really didn't care what was on, just so long as the apartment wasn't too quiet.

Pulling the buns off a leftover cheeseburger, he crumbled the meat, cheese, onions, and condiments into a bowl of raw, scrambled eggs. These he cooked together until they congealed into something solid, and he added a little salt. Sitting with the plate on his lap, he half-watched some black and white footage of oil drilling in Texas.

Just then, Brynn walked by his door with her long legs bare, wearing a long-sleeve white shirt. Was she naked from the waist down? She came back by. She was wearing skimpy underwear, not quite as small as a thong, and a shirt. She was out on the balcony, street side. The third time she came by, she glanced in.

"Oh, hi!" she said.

Was she kidding? "Hi Brynn," Tom said, turning back to the TV and taking a bite of his cheeseburger omelet.

"What are you eating?" she asked.

"Breakfast," he said, without looking away from the TV. He wasn't a prude; he just didn't want to reward her weird behavior. He wanted to deny her the shocked look. *She did have nice legs, though.*

"It's going to be another warm day," she said.

"Then why the long-sleeves?" he asked.

"You want to see more of me, don't you?" she asked.

He looked at her; she was smiling, and leaning against his door again. He said, "It's just too warm for long sleeves."

"You feeling warm, Tom?"

"Whatever. Wear long sleeves then," he said.

"The sleeves cover my scars. I used to cut," she said.

"Cut?"

"You know, cut myself. Up and down my arms, the scars are ugly, but yesterday was my six-month anniversary," she said.

"Anniversary of what?"

"Of *not* cutting," she said.

He looked back to the television, and took another bite of his omelet. "Cutting, like a suicide attempt?"

She opened the door and stepped in.

"You didn't know me well enough a couple days ago, but now you come in wearing underwear?" Tom asked.

She pulled up one sleeve, revealing a dozen parallel lines cut crosswise, running up her arm and disappearing under the sleeve.

"Not suicide attempts, just cuts. A lot of people cut," she said.

"Why?"

She hesitated. "To prove they can still feel. Still bleed. To be in control of something. Lots of reasons."

"But then they wear long-sleeves?"

"Or long pants," she said.

"People cut their legs, too?"

"I never have. I like my legs. A lot of cutters cut on their upper ribcage so it is less likely to be seen by anyone," she said.

He took another bite. *Why was she telling him all this?* He asked, "What does your boyfriend think?"

"I don't have one. I lied before. But seriously, quitting cutting is like quitting any addiction."

"You can get addicted to cutting?"

She said, "Fuck, yeah. It's a tough addiction to beat."

He took another bite and focused on the TV. A silence set in with Brynn standing there, half-naked, the scars on one arm exposed, and Tom eating his cheeseburger omelet, watching a Swiffer commercial. Neither said anything until Brynn turned to leave.

"Whatever," she said and walked out. Tom glanced at her, watching her go. *A damn shame, really.*

The door slammed and Tom changed the channel. Ben soon appeared in the doorway.

Ben asked, "Are you fucking Brynn? That's bad news, man, don't do it. She's crazy."

"I'm not," Tom said.

"She just bailed out of your apartment with her bare ass in the wind," Ben said.

"I didn't even invite her in. She showed up like that, showed me her scars, and then took off," Tom said.

"She's targeting you. Keep resisting, man. She's psycho. She tries to kill herself all the time," Ben said.

"The cuts aren't suicide attempts, she told me. She also says that she hasn't cut in six months," Tom said.

"That may be, but she was in an ambulance two weeks ago because of pills. She left a note. In the past year, she's probably been rushed to the hospital twenty times by one of us or by an ambulance," Ben said.

Tom looked at Ben. "Did you sleep with her?"

"I did, but that was before I knew, man. She's *loco*. When I 'broke up' with her after a three-day affair, we had to talk her off her railing," Ben said. He was pointing upward to Brynn's apartment. "I'm trying to spare you."

"There was never any real danger to me, Ben," Tom said. He took his last bite of omelet. "But thanks for the heads-up. I'll lock my door more often."

"And don't fuck her," Ben said.

"Right," Tom said.

A voice from behind Ben called out, "Hey, is the new guy sleeping with Brynn?"

Ben looked back. Tom couldn't see who it was.

Ben said, "Hey, Mike. He says he's not."

Mike appeared in the doorway beside Ben, and said, "Don't do it. She's nuts."

Tom heard the door above as it suddenly slid open, and then Brynn shouted down, "I'm not fucking any of you! Stop talking about me!"

Ben and Mike looked up.

Mike said, "Aw, girl, put some clothes on."

Tom heard Brynn's footsteps and then her door slammed shut. *This place is the Cuckoo's Nest.*

"Leave her alone," a young woman's voice came up from below.

"We didn't do anything," Mike said.

"It's all good, Winnie. She was just walking around in her underwear, and we thought maybe she was fucking the new guy," Ben said.

"Aw, gross," Winnie said.

Gross? Tom wondered if Winnie had even seen him yet. *How could he already be labeled as gross?*

"Like I said, it's all good," Ben said.

Brynn's door pulled open again. "Shut *up!*" she screeched and then slammed her door once again.

"We'll be calling 911 tonight, sure as shit," Mike said, looking up.

They didn't have to call 911 that night, but Tom decided he might need to find a different place to live.

3

His first official day at the *Portage Herald* was a Wednesday, which was the easiest day of the week because the latest issue had hit newsstands that morning, and so the staff had a whole week to put together the next issue.

Dennis Brontil was the editor, and Tom was one of two reporters. There were two sales people, a receptionist, a business manager, her assistant, and two layout people. The company owned its own presses in a print shop at the far end of the parking lot, so they didn't have to send the paper out to a third party for printing.

Tom felt unexpectedly nervous. Sure, it was a new job working with people he didn't know very well, not to mention a new community to get familiar with, but he'd done this work for years. Still, somehow, things felt different, almost as if there were some element of risk. Walking into the office that first time, Tom had a flash-sense that his life was on a course to additional upheaval. So much so, he stopped in the entryway, and considered going home. Shaking it off, he walked on. He'd already lost Vicky, his dog, and his house. What else could he lose?

Behind a grey partition, Tom found two desks facing each other. One impossibly cluttered, the other empty except for a laptop. He placed his bag on the empty one. There was a single unframed window, two-foot square, five feet above the floor. The walls were a faded plum color. Allan Morrison, the paper's other reporter, stepped in behind him and said, "Morning."

They had met at Tom's interview. Allan shared that he had moved to Portage twenty years before from upstate New York, working first as a dorm parent in a school for troubled boys, and then at the local recreation department, before finally joining the *Herald*. His hair was greying, his glasses were thick, and he gave the impression of a man who was frustrated with how boring life was.

"Morning," Tom said.

Allan sat behind the cluttered desk, and Tom sat at the empty one. His laptop had not fully booted up before Brontil strolled in.

"Settling in?" Brontil said.

Allan sighed.

Tom said, "Just beginning to."

"Good, good," Brontil said. "Are you living in Portage?"

Tom said, "I found an apartment on Highland Street."

"On Highland?" Brontil asked, his brow wrinkling.

"Nice place?" Allan asked.

"It's okay," Tom said. "The neighbors are a bit wacky. Had a twenty-something walking around on the shared balcony in her underwear last weekend."

Brontil said, "Oh, like a wild college apartment sort of place?"

"She's not a student. She used to cut herself, she tells me. She wanders, scantily clad, into other people apartments," Tom said. "She's not the only character there, either. There seems to be quite a collection."

Allan asked, "Are there a lot of students in the building? In the other apartments?"

"From what I know so far, only one is a student. There's a married couple, a few retirees, and two brothers who hang drywall for a living," Tom said.

Brontil said, "Oh! The Lennox brothers."

"You know them?" Tom asked.

Brontil said, "Sure, sure."

"You're living in the Cooper apartments?" Allan asked.

"Is that bad?" Tom asked.

Allan asked, "Want us to help you find something else?"

"I was thinking that maybe I'd look around," Tom said.

"That place is a bit much. There are stories in there for sure," Brontil said.

"That one kid alone—she calls herself 'Brynn'—would be an interesting story," Tom said.

"So, write them," Brontil said.

Allan winced, and he ran a hand through his grey hair.

"Well, I don't know…" Tom said.

"How many apartments are over there, like, eight?" Brontil asked.

"Nine in all," Tom said.

"So, eight plus you? You could write a feature per week on the Cooper Building residents," Brontil said.

"But I live there," Tom said.

"Get their perspectives on Portage, and what it's like to be a local. You mentioned retirees; they'll have a long view on the history of the town. Spend time with them, and get a new perspective each week. But not *too* edgy, don't forget," Brontil said.

Allan said, through nearly clenched teeth, "Refrigerator news."

"Refrigerator news?" Tom asked.

"You know, news that people clip out and hang on the fridge door with a magnet. That's primarily what we do here. If people want the nasty details, they can go to the dailies. We can't scoop anyone anyway. But we can write thoughtful pieces that people want to share," Brontil said.

It sounded horrible to Tom; "refrigerator news" wasn't mentioned in the interview, and the last weekly he worked for actually did scoop the daily newspapers now and then.

"Refrigerator news," Allan said, and then winked. Tom could tell Allan hated it, too, but that he had little fight left in him.

"See what you can come up with by Monday," Brontil said, before strolling out.

Tom looked across at Allan. "The lunatic upstairs attempts suicide on a regular basis to garner attention, and she's the most interesting one of the bunch."

Allan said, "I don't think you have much choice. Look, you're being paid to write. A lot of people wish they could do that."

Tom would have to spend hours with each of his neighbors; maybe he could simply slip a survey under each door.

"These people probably lead dull lives. You can make them feel special for a little while," Allan said.

Tom hadn't really considered the 'lives of quiet desperation' angle.

"But if you really don't want to do it, make the first one terribly boring," Allan suggested. "Maybe Dennis will kill the assignment."

Tom shook his head. His first assignment was a series of features. Not a drug bust, not local politics, and not even a ribbon cutting. Instead, a series… on his neighbors.

4

He had considered interviewing Brynn first, but he was concerned that she might be strange enough to be interesting. So instead, he decided to interview Marie, the older woman who lived alone in apartment 1B, directly below him.

She welcomed him in, and offered him a seat on the couch. It was pleather, and draped with a brown and orange afghan blanket. Every horizontal surface Tom could see was bare; he placed a small recorder on the coffee table. Tom expected to see a cat, or a few cats, appear at any moment, but none did. The place smelled like a lilac-scented candle had just been blown out.

Tom asked, "You're sure this is a good time for a little chat?"

Marie said, "I've lived here for twelve years. I've seen everybody come and go. All except for old Mr. Hitch. And the town's changed *so* much, that's for sure."

"Before we really get started, would you mind stating your name and age, please?" Tom asked.

She leaned forward, staring at the recorder, and said, "Marie Dupuis, and I'm sixty-six years old." She then looked up at Tom, apparently seeking his approval.

"Fine. So, I want you to just tell me about yourself. The story I'm writing will try to convey a picture of who you are, and by knowing you a bit better, we'll learn something about the community," Tom said.

"Oh, well, I'm sure there isn't enough about me to fill a story," she said.

Tom agreed, there probably wasn't even a lead paragraph here. What could the lady say? Something like, 'I've spent sixty-six years in a small town, got married, raised a kid, got widowed, and now spend my time watching Family Feud reruns'?

Marie said, "I go to the Episcopal church on Main Street."

Tom wanted to die.

Marie said, "And I believe we are all descendants of aliens."

What the fuck did she just say?

Marie said, "Oh, and I remember when the girls in the coffee shop used to pour your coffee for you."

"I'm sorry, wait, what?" Tom asked.

"Those girls, in the coffee shop, when they stop fixing their hair and texting their friends, they take your money but they don't even pour your coffee. They just hand you an empty paper cup and you go fill it yourself. It's like getting coffee at the bus station or a hospital waiting room. And the furniture is dirty, and the layout of that place is just awful, I mean…"

"About the aliens?" Tom said.

"Oh, right. We are all descendants of ancient aliens who came here and cross-bred with monkeys in order to develop our race," she said.

Holy shit.

Proceeding cautiously, Tom asked, "Why exactly would they do that?"

Marie laughed. "Well, I'm sure I don't know. We'll find out someday, though."

Teasing a bit, Tom said, "Maybe it was to create a race of slaves."

Marie dismissed this out of hand. "Beings advanced enough to come all this way and carefully breed a new race would not have the institution of slavery. Besides, you don't breed slaves. You capture them. They would have found slaves on another world, and they'd be harder working and more powerful than we are. I mean, really, they wouldn't need slaves. I'm sure there are intergalactic Mexicans who are willing to do work that original residents of the home planet won't do."

Was she kidding?

"Marie, when did you start believing all this?" Tom asked.

"First time I heard it. It just made sense," she said. "I mean, does it make sense to you that a bunch of people whose most advanced technology was the chariot could crack a few whips and get a bunch of Hebrew slaves to build three pyramids?"

Tom asked, "You mean, is it more believable than aliens?"

"Exactly. That's my point. Of course, it's more likely that aliens built them. I mean, they had a river that flooded every year, and they also had famine. If those people were able to build the pyramids, wouldn't they have built dams and other things to control the river instead of spending all that time and effort constructing tombs?"

"Why would aliens want pyramids?" Tom asked.

"Navigation aids or something, I don't know. Maybe some sort of antenna array to contact them once we got smart enough to figure out how to use them," she said.

"But until then, we buried people in them?" Tom asked.

"There are people in the piers of the Golden Gate Bridge," she said.

Tom said, "They're there by accident."

Marie paused, blinked, and then asked, "You don't actually believe that, do you?"

Tom backed up. "What do you think the aliens would think of our society today?"

"Which society? I never know what people mean by that. How can the word 'society' mean women in the Amazon who worry about feeding their kids as a group—you know like a village, like Hillary said—while at the same time 'society' means those self-centered women who act like children, like I saw on *Sex in the City*? I mean, that Carrie Bradshaw lady didn't actually deserve any of those guys, you know? Especially Aiden, he was so nice, but not even Mr. Big. No woman in my day would've respected those girls. So, I'm not sure which society the aliens would find, or what they would think," she said.

"Maybe we'll evolve a bit more before they return," Tom said.

Marie stood. "The coffee must be ready. How do you like yours?"

"Black with a bit of sugar," Tom said.

"Be right back," Marie said, and walked off into the kitchen. Tom looked down at the recorder. Could he write this story? It would make her the target of a lot of teasing at the supermarket, the coffee shop, and the salon. He glanced out the window just in time to see an older, portly man in an orange and black wetsuit crossing the parking lot toward the stairs.

Marie returned then and, seeing the man as well, she said, "That's Mr. Hitch." Setting two cups of coffee between them, she sat, but didn't offer an explanation or even speculation about the man in the wetsuit. Tom didn't ask.

"Thank you," Tom said. "Now, does anyone else know that you believe we're descended from aliens?"

"Oh, everyone knows," she said.

"They do?" Tom asked.

"I tell people every chance I get," Marie said.

"My concern is that if I include it in the story…"

"That people will think I'm crazy?" Marie asked. "Let them. When the aliens return, I'll be proven right. And if they come back after I'm in the boneyard, well, then it won't matter, will it?"

Tom smiled. He loved how New Englanders talked when you got away from the cities. Marie wasn't crazy, Tom knew. He'd seen the same theory on the History Channel, and thousands probably believed just as she did. He just couldn't imagine why an intelligent race would choose Earth. It was so far out of the way.

"Is there anything else you'd like to add?" Tom asked.

"Yes, I wonder if anyone has seen Elvis lately," she said.

There was an awkward moment, but then Marie howled with laughter and asked, "Boy, you'll believe just about anything, won't you?"

"Wait, you were kidding?" Tom asked.

"Well, of course," she said.

"Oh God, you really had me going with the aliens thing," Tom said.

Marie immediately became serious, "Oh no, I meant what I said about aliens; I was only joking about Elvis."

Tom watched for some clue that she was kidding, and waited for her to laugh again, but she didn't.

"I'm dead serious about the aliens," she said.

"Okay," Tom said.

"I shouldn't have joked about Elvis, because now you're all unsure of yourself," she said.

"No, it's alright. And I can still tell people what you believe about the aliens?" Tom asked.

"Like I said, everybody already knows," she said.

Tom slowly stood, and said, "Thank you for your time, Marie."

"Thanks for coming by," Marie said.

Tom headed for the door.

5

The next day, as Tom climbed the stairs toward the 2ⁿᵈ floor balcony, a woman spoke to him from beneath the stairs.

"Why are you writing stories about us?" she asked.

Tom looked through the wrought-iron steps, and saw a person who appeared devoid of all color.

"You're Winnie?" he asked.

"Why are you writing stories? Doesn't Big Brother have enough data on each of us already? You want to make our lives part of the public record?"

"I don't have to interview you," Tom asked.

"Then what? You'll report that?" she asked. Her voice was soft; it wasn't like she was some nut, howling at him. Instead, she seemed legitimately concerned. Her hair looked like corn silk, and her skin was impossibly pale. Her eyes were cyan, set in blonde eyelashes. She was very thin, and the pale dress she wore was simple, as if a cylinder of cloth had been hemmed on one end and sewn with shoulder straps on the other. Tom was beginning to doubt that any woman in the building, except Marie, bothered to wear a bra.

"I won't report anything you don't want me to," he said. He thought he might explain what refrigerator news was, but then decided against it.

"But what's your purpose, you know?" she asked.

Good question. To serve the public? To bring unbiased reporting to the readers? To bring useful news to the masses?

"I'm willing to compare our contributions to the planet," Tom said. *Ugh. Why'd he say that?*

Winnie stepped forward. "I'm willing to look at what we both contribute, as long as you're also willing to talk about what we each *take* from the planet, and to compare our footprints."

Tom said, "I don't really have the time."

"Aw man, c'mon, of course you do. That's *all* you've got," she said, smiling.

Without responding, Tom climbed up to the balcony, and went to his apartment. But then, suddenly, he spun around, headed back to the stairs, and down to apartment 1C. He knocked, and Winnie appeared on the other side of the screen door.

"Come to dinner with me," Tom said.

"Where?" she asked.

"How about Betterman's?"

Winnie looked at him a minute and then said, "I'm not going anywhere with you."

"Look, you don't know me, but I can't be as bad as you think I am," Tom said.

"I won't go out with you, but I'll cook for you here," she said.

"You will?" Tom asked.

"Come back around dinner time," she said.

"What time is that?"

"Around 8pm."

"You eat late," Tom said.

"Everyone else eats too early," she said. She pulled a few loose strands of nearly white hair from her white face. She moved gracefully and blinked slowly.

"Okay, see you then," Tom said. "Can I bring anything?"

Smiling, she said, "Please don't." She faded backward into the shadow and closed the inner door. Tom grinned and climbed the stairs once more, finding Ben on the balcony, smoking a pipe. The unmistakable odor of weed hung heavy and dank. Ben smiled, and offered to share.

"Never before lunch," Tom said. "Thanks anyway."

"Have a date with Winnie, huh?" Ben asked.

There was no privacy here. Tom asked, "Should I avoid sleeping with her, too?"

"By all means, if you can get some of that, do it," Ben said. "Good luck to you."

The door opened above, and Brynn looked down on them from her balcony. She asked, "What are you guys talking about?"

"Tom is going to Winnie's for supper," Ben said.

Tom winced when Brynn said, "Figures. Enjoy your bean sprouts and lemongrass shake." She disappeared from sight, and the men heard her door close.

Ben held a finger to his lips and then pointed upward, indicating that she might have closed the door but remained outside to eavesdrop. Tom nodded.

"What did she mean by 'lemongrass shake'? Is Winnie a vegetarian?" Tom asked.

"A *vegan,* man. And she's all up in the politics of it. More angry than philosophical, sometimes, if you know what I mean. You shouldn't even wear a leather belt, dude. Not worth the hassle. Just let your pants fall. Might even work out," Ben said.

"Does she sleep around?" Tom asked.

"Winnie? No way, man. I'm not even sure if that kinda meat isn't off her menu, too, you know what I mean?"

"Nah, Ben, too subtle. I didn't get it," Tom said, rolling his eyes.

"Besides, she's just a kid."

Ben said, "Not really, she just turned thirty last year or something like that. Sure you don't want some?" He offered the pipe again.

"Pretty sure," Tom said. "I have to write up the interview with Marie this afternoon."

"Do you go into the office at all, man?"

"As little as possible. Especially on Thursday and Friday, but on Monday and Tuesday, I really can't avoid it," Tom said.

Mike and Matt Lennox, the drywall brothers, came out of their apartment. To Ben, Mike said, "You smoking that shit again? No wonder you can't motivate."

Matt said, "Come hang some drywall with us," and the brothers laughed.

"You guys go ahead, hang your drywall, and play with mud. I'll go make some fries later. Everyone will be happy," Ben said, smiling.

"How 'bout you, Tom? Want to earn some honest money?" Matt asked.

Ben replied before Tom could. "He can't. Winnie's making him dinner later."

All three of them were laughing before Tom could say a word.

"Aw man, come *make* sawdust with us instead of *eating* sawdust with her," Matt said.

"She'll never sleep with you, man. You smell too much like soap," Mike said.

Brynn suddenly appeared above. "There's more to women than fucking you know!"

Having no idea she might be up there, the brothers were startled, and Ben laughed in a way that only cannabis makes possible. Tom couldn't help but laugh, too.

"Shit! Get back, witch!" Matt shouted, holding his hands up, with index fingers crossed like a crucifix.

"Fuck you!" Brynn said, and then she was gone again. They heard her door open and slam closed.

Mike and Matt, still laughing, headed for the stairs.

"Well, see ya," Tom said, walking to his door.

"Yep," Ben said, holding smoke.

Once inside, Tom looked around and sighed. He had the piece on Marie to write, but wanted to clear some of the screaming and laughing out of his ears, and the smoke from his nose. The story had the potential to be silly enough as it was. He had decided he'd try to make Marie as sympathetic as possible, to show her as a loveable type, the sort of wacky great-aunt everyone enjoys. He grabbed the laptop from the end table, created a blank document, and began writing:

"Marie Dupuis is a widow living alone in her Portage apartment, serving tea and coffee to guests, and she believes we are descendants of ancient aliens."

Okay, so that didn't make her as sympathetic as he'd hoped. AP Style really didn't lend itself to extensive character development. He had to drop all the important information on the reader in the first sentence.

"To any visitor, she would seem the sweet and ordinary sort of woman you would love to spend an afternoon with, but she quickly becomes much more interesting than one would expect. There are many people who believe the idea that ancient aliens visited Earth many thousands of years ago, and that many of our technological feats, from architecture to medicine, were actually made possible by extraterrestrial help."

He sat back, looked out on the balcony, and Ben was gone. Tom wished he had taken him up on his offer. *Would Brontil want this story this way? Was this still refrigerator news?* He'd write it and see.

6

Later that evening, around 8pm, Tom arrived at Winnie's apartment. He wore shorts and a button-down, short-sleeved shirt, untucked. He even managed to find a pair of sandals.

He knocked at the door, and when it opened, Winnie was wearing a dress one might wear to a summer wedding. Her hair was up, and she was wearing low heals. The two of them together looked like a woman opening the door for the man who was to clean her pool. They laughed.

"Did you dress up for me?" she asked, smiling, and showed him in. She immediately stepped out of her shoes, took down her hair, and stepped out of the room. When she returned, she asked, "Are you hungry?"

"I could eat," Tom said.

"Good. I hope you like bean sprouts and wheatgrass shakes," she said.

"Jesus, can everyone hear everything in this place? And why don't I ever hear anything?" Tom asked.

"Because you're not really listening yet," she said, and went to the stove. "Have a seat wherever you like."

Tom said, "Some of that conversation was pretty embarrassing."

Tom sat on a small loveseat in the living room. There were

many plants, and no television. There were many books, but no sign of a Kindle. The one phone he saw was connected to the wall.

"Put on some music if you like," Winnie said.

There was an iPhone, connected to a couple of speakers. Tom lifted it, and dialed up a playlist titled, "Cool music." The first song was by a band he'd never heard of.

He read the name aloud, "Whiskey Geese?"

"A duo—bluesy soul stuff—from New England," she said.

It was acoustic and, as promised, cool.

She said, "You ever heard of Po Boyz or Otis Grove?"

He asked, "Are they up next?"

"No, the members of those two got together and... never mind," she said. "Would you have a glass of wine?"

"With dinner?" Tom asked.

"Or before. Whatever you'd like," she said.

"I'll have a glass," he said, heading to the kitchen.

"Good. Pour me one too, please," Winnie said. She pointed to a blue bottle on the counter.

He poured wine into two large glasses, stopping too soon for her.

"Do it up," she said, pointing at the glasses.

The kitchen smelled great, like onions and garlic. She added some sort of thick liquid.

"Honey?" Tom asked.

She raised a slender finger in objection. "It's Bee-Free Honee."

"How do you make honey without bees?" he asked.

"Apparently, by chance, with apples. A woman came up with it by accident with a failed batch of apple jelly," she said. Winnie put a little on her fingertip and extended it. "Try it."

Tom's eyebrows went up.

"Just getting you to try something new," she said.

Tom stepped closer, and took her finger into his mouth. The Bee-Free Honee was sweeter than the real stuff, but not overpowering.

"What do you think?" she asked.

He smiled, and said, "Good. What are you making?"

"Steak," she said, and giggled.

"Ugh, sick!" Tom said, and handed her a glass of wine.

She raised her glass and said, "To humor."

"To interesting people," he said.

The wine was also sweet. She dished a couple servings of dinner, turned with a plate in each hand, and moved to the small table.

"Isn't that chicken?" he asked.

"Tofu. It's Kung Pao Tofu. Let's try it," she said.

They sat. He sniffed at a large chunk of red bell pepper.

"Sweet and spicy," she said, and took a bite.

She was right. The tofu wasn't nearly as mushy as he thought it might be. In fact, Tom was impressed, and he lifted his glass again. "Delicious."

She raised hers. "Corny. But sweet."

They ate, they discussed how their politics differed, and did so amicably, without hyperbole, and with as few 'they say' citations as possible. They discussed the newspaper and modern journalism, they discussed the bookshop where she worked, and her studies at the university. When dinner and three bottles of wine were behind them, they'd had a near-perfect evening. Tom couldn't remember the last time he'd had such a simple and happy time.

She was *too* perfect. "So, why isn't there a Mr. Winnie?" he asked.

She paused, her smile fell a bit, and then she said, "There was. Miles and I were very much in love. We were married about ten months, and we attended a party. I left early. Had to get to bed, but I didn't want to ruin his fun, so I got a ride home with a girl friend who was also leaving. Miles never made it home."

Tom waited, and then asked, "Can I ask?"

"Miles had quite a bit more to drink. Then after midnight, he tried to drive. His car went into a ditch, flipped over, and he was killed," she said, staring at the table.

"Oh God, I'm so sorry," Tom said, feeling as though he'd ruined the evening.

"It was years ago, so I've found a place to put him, and my memories, but thank you," she said. "And how about you? No Mrs. Tom?"

"My last relationship lasted almost ten years. It ended when I couldn't convince myself anymore that she wasn't cheating on me," Tom said.

"You caught her?" Winnie said.

"You lie to yourself, you know?" Tom said. "I mean, I'd find a clue, and when I'd ask her about it, she'd say only, 'I don't know why that's like that,' or whatever."

"Ouch," Winnie said.

"I convinced myself it was okay, that it was just weird things that happen," Tom said.

"Really?" Winnie asked.

"I did," Tom said.

"Ah, yeah, seems like she felt at least a little guilt," she said.

"It gets worse. About three days later, I found a man's wedding ring on the floor of the car," Tom said.

"Someone else felt guilty, too. What did she say about the ring?" Winnie said.

"I didn't confront her. Instead, I carried it in my wallet for years. I got used to it being there. Besides, it was way too small for me, so I took some comfort in the fact that I could probably beat him to death," Tom said.

Winnie chuckled, but then caught herself.

"No, it's okay to laugh," Tom said. "It's been a while. I was sitting next to her, a couple years before, when she received an email from a male coworker that called her 'sweetheart' and mentioned taking her out on a boat."

"How was she able to explain *that* away?" Winnie asked.

Tom paused, and then said, "Because I let her."

There was an awkward silence, and then Tom said, "Well, I should go."

"Aw, it's okay, we can change the subject," Winnie said.

"I'm tired," he said, and rose to leave. She walked him to the door, stood on her toes, and kissed his cheek.

"Thanks for a fun time, Winnie," Tom said.

"Not bad, huh?" she asked, winking.

"It was great," he said, and stepped out into the dark.

She said, "Goodnight."

The air was cool and sweet. He wished that they hadn't talked about Vicky, or even Miles. He shook his head, and then Tom glimpsed the back of Mr. Hitch as he was leaving the parking lot and walking down the street. *A plaid shirt and cowboy boots?* Tom turned and climbed the stairs to his balcony, but he didn't see Brynn until he looked up with his key in hand.

"Dating the albino anorexic freak now, are we?" Brynn asked.

"Just had dinner, Brynn," he said. He tried to pass her, but she sidestepped into his path.

"Why don't guys ever just want to have dinner with me?" Brynn asked.

"Maybe you're just looking to the wrong set of guys," he said.

She swayed a bit, and leaned against the loose railing. Tom stepped forward.

"Ooh, did that make you nervous?" she asked.

"Did what make me nervous?" Tom asked, while trying again to step past her. He wanted to get into his apartment, to have an evening that was about Winnie and dinner, and not about Brynn. She moved quickly and stood in his doorway, hand over the keyhole.

"You're just another one of *them*. You'd fuck me if I gave you half a chance, but you don't care about me as a person. You don't really care," she said. "I mean, when was the last time you wondered what I was doing, how I was?"

Tom didn't like her tone, or her body language. She wasn't screaming this time; she was speaking as if discussing a disturbing and thought-provoking film. If she were fully immersed in her drama, what were the limits?

"I do care and I do wonder. In fact, I finished writing a feature on Marie today, and I was hoping I could write your story next," he said.

"God. Does that work on people? That condescending tone, speaking to me as if I were a kid?" she asked.

Tom said, "No, I'm serious. Why don't you go upstairs, get some sleep, and we can work on it tomorrow morning?" He placed his hands on her shoulders, and she was even more unsteady than she appeared. Brynn suddenly lunged forward and kissed Tom; her strawberry-wine tongue plunged into his mouth before he could push her away.

Slapping him, she nearly fell in the effort. He grabbed her around the middle to steady her and she screamed, "Don't touch me, you pervert!" She struggled to be free, but Tom sensed if he released her, she would drop at his feet. She struck him again and again, shrieking. Mike came out of his apartment, and then Ben came out behind Tom.

"What the hell?" Ben asked.

Brynn broke free of Tom's grip and, still howling, leapt over the railing, disappearing from Tom's sight. The three men rushed forward and looked down. Brynn was conscious and rolling around on the pavement below. Strangely, she was silent now. Winnie was the first to reach her, and Mike was already dialing his cell phone. A middle-aged man on a unicycle suddenly appeared. He had long straight hair, fuzz on his face, was shirtless, with a cigarette hanging from one lip. Tom had heard of him, the resident of apartment 1A; his name was Miguel something.

"Call an ambulance!" Winnie said.

"They're on the way!" Mike shouted back.

Miguel jumped off the unicycle and ran to Brynn's side. He asked, "Did she fall, or jump on purpose?" Winnie didn't answer.

Tom, Ben, and Mike ran down and joined the others by Brynn's side, and she took Mike's hand and squeezed it tight.

"You'll be okay," Tom said.

Within five minutes, a siren could be heard, fast approaching. Soon after, the ambulance came into the lot and halted close by. The EMTs looked upward as they approached, guessing from where Brynn had come. "What happened?"

"She fell," Mike said.

"Where does it hurt?"

"I think it's her hip," Winnie said.

"What's your name?" the younger of the EMTs asked.

"This is Brynn," the senior EMT said.

Brynn was back-boarded and placed on a gurney. As they were loading her, she turned to Tom. "Will you come?" The younger

EMT entered the rear of the ambulance.

"I'll meet you there," Tom said. He turned to the older EMT and asked, "Which hospital?"

The EMT closed the doors of the ambulance and said, "There's only one." He then walked to the cab and drove away. Lights, no siren.

"Did she jump?" Miguel asked again.

"She ran right over the railing," Mike said.

Miguel looked up. "She wasn't serious, then. About suicide, I mean. Not until the 3rd floor or higher. This is a cry for help."

"Spontaneous," Tom said.

"Right on," Ben said. "Totally spur of the moment. No planning. I bet if that had been the tenth floor, she woulda gone."

"Spontaneous, huh?" Miguel said. "I bet she was working on suicidal ideation for a while, like given the right circumstances with the right audience with the right heightened sense of drama, she was going to go."

He didn't know much about Miguel. It seemed unlikely, with the unicycle, but Tom had to ask. "Are you a psychologist?" *Maybe a student?*

"I'm a schizophrenic. The voices tell me to do stuff like that all the time, but the difference with Brynn is she does it," said Miguel.

"She's schizophrenic?" Tom asked.

"Not exactly. Instead of voices, she follows the soap opera script she sees in her head," Miguel said.

"Does she have family we should call?" Tom asked.

"No one who will come," Ben said.

7

When Tom arrived at the counter, the nurse never looked up. Her hair was streaked with grey and appeared tourniquet-tight at the back of her head.

"Are you a relative?"

"I'm the closest thing she'll have showing up tonight," he said.

She stopped writing briefly, still did not look up, and said, "Please have a seat, I'll let you know when you can see her."

"Will she be admitted?" Tom asked.

"No idea yet, sir. She's still in radiology," she said. She clipped three pages together. "I'll let you know when you can see her."

He sat down beside an elderly couple. The couple sat, silently holding each other, and every few minutes the gentleman coughed ever so softly and, each time, his wife rubbed his arm. Tom wondered if anyone ever fell in love like that anymore.

A few seats down, a man slept in a blue cotton work jacket. On his chest, a white patch had "Jared" embroidered in red script. Tom looked around for a magazine, but only found a discarded and folded copy of last Wednesday's *Portage Herald*. Refrigerator news. Well, actually, there was a bit of hard news. On the front page, above the fold, there were three columns for a story about a local thirty-year-old man who stole a car, drove drunk over to an ex-girlfriend's home, exposed himself to her and her mother, and then led police on a chase that lasted nearly fifteen minutes and took him out onto the highway, then ended in a drainage ditch near Walmart.

Flipping through, there were stories about the local fire department winning best overall at a regional muster, a local man who won second place in a competition for loggers, and a couple who owned lakefront property and were petitioning to secede from the town of Portage. There were photos of pre-teen beauty queens, wildlife, and of various certificates being awarded.

Jared farted in his sleep, waking himself, just as the nurse called Tom over.

"You can see her. She's asking if you're here. Room 3, right there on the left."

"Thank you," Tom said, crossed the hallway, and entered Room 3. He found Brynn in a hospital johnnie, lying on paper, with a sheet over her. They had started an IV in the back of her left hand. Tom guessed it was in part for pain medication, because Brynn seemed quite comfortable. She even smiled when she saw him.

"How are you doing?" Tom asked.

"Pretty good for someone who fell from a 2nd floor balcony," she said.

Fell.

"Did they tell you anything yet?" he asked.

"They suspect I bruised my pelvis," she said. "They want to make sure there's no fracture."

Tom winced.

"I guess we won't be hooking up anytime soon," she said and smiled broadly.

Then a young woman arrived and said, "I'm Dr. Lendell. How are you feeling?"

"Super," Brynn said.

"Well the good news is there are no broken bones. It seems it's only a deep bruise. You're going to be sore for a while. I'll write you a script for the pain," Lendell said. Then of Tom she asked, "Are you Dad?"

Brynn began to chuckle, a drowsy half-hearted laugh.

"I'm a neighbor. She asked me to come," he said. "Tom Tibbetts."

Lendell said to Brynn, "Can you tell me how you fell?"

Brynn said only, "Gravity," and she laughed again.

Lendell's face set and she took Tom aside. "I don't know how much you know about her, and I'd rather be talking to a family member, but she's got signs of self-destructive behavior, scars that look like cutting. Are you familiar with it?"

"She showed me," Tom said. "And tonight she suddenly ran and jumped over the railing; she didn't just fall from that balcony."

"Any diagnoses of mental illness that you know of?" Lendell asked.

"Only by the resident schizophrenic in our building," Tom said. "Doesn't she have medical records here? I'm told she has a long history of coming here. She must have a file a couple inches thick."

Lendell didn't seem to have much of a sense of humor.

"Look, I'm not sure if I can discharge her. I'm not convinced that she is not an immediate threat to herself," Lendell said.

Tom said, "I'm convinced she *is* a threat to herself. What can I do?"

"Is there someone that can stay with her tonight?" Lendell asked.

"Here at the hospital?" Tom asked.

"If I release her, is there someone who might stay with her, to keep an eye on her?" Lendell asked.

Tom looked at Brynn, who seemed drug-happy. *How tough could it be?*

"Will she be medicated?" Tom asked.

"I'll give her something for pain," Lendell said.

Tom looked at her again, and then at the floor, and his shoes. He sighed.

"I could take her home," he said.

"Let's keep her here for a couple more hours, and then I'll release her with a script," Lendell said.

"Will I be able to go to work in the morning?" Tom asked, but Dr. Lendell was already out of the room and headed down the hallway.

* * *

The drive home was quiet. Brynn stared out the car window. Tom wasn't sure her eyes were tracking the lights drifting by. When they got to the apartment building, Tom could see Matt Lennox loading the bed of their pickup truck. He had the quick, furtive movements one would expect from an amateur drug dealer. Tom decided to treat him that way and ignored him. He wasn't sure Brynn had seen them.

Tom and Brynn began navigating the stairs to the second balcony. She was compliant, and a bit too pliant. With each step, her rubbery legs buckled a fraction of an inch. Tom wondered if she'd wake from the fog when she saw the balcony from where she had leapt, but she didn't. She glanced that way, gave it a half-hearted second look, and then they turned up the stairs to reach Brynn's floor. They hadn't gotten more than a couple steps when Mike Lennox appeared at the top. He seemed surprised.

"You okay?" Mike asked.

"I'll be fine," she said.

Mike hesitated, as if unsure, and then simply nodded. He came down past them without another word, and then continued down to the parking lot.

Tom and Brynn climbed the remaining steps. When they got to her door, Tom asked, "Where are the keys?"

"It's open," she said.

Of course it is. Tom pushed the door open and then helped Brynn through it. He turned on a light revealing a surprisingly normal-looking living room. Tom had expected the walls to be painted glossy black and Pepto-Bismol pink. Instead, the walls were pastel yellow, with an accent wall, and large healthy plants in each corner.

He helped her to her bedroom, and this room was also tastefully and simply decorated. He guided her to the bed.

"Can you go in the drawer, second from the top? Grab me a pair of pajama pants," she said, sounding exhausted. Tom found the cotton pants, tossed them onto the bed, and said, "I have to go down and get your meds out of the car."

"I'll change," she said.

Tom returned to the parking lot, and retrieved the medication and her phone. The Lennox brothers were still milling around their pickup, tying down a tarp over the bed. When they spotted Tom watching them, both brothers froze for a moment. Tom left them behind, climbed back to Brynn's floor, and entered the apartment without knocking, but he tapped on her bedroom door before walking in. Brynn was lying on her bed, pajama pants on, atop the bedspread. Tom put the pills and her phone on the nightstand, and took a long scanning look at Brynn, from her toes to her eyes.

"I should go, just call if you need anything," Tom said.

"Please stay," she said.

"Brynn," he said.

"It's not a horizontal proposition. I'm just saying, we'll sleep. I'm afraid of waking up in the middle of the night in crazy pain, and being alone," she said, her voice soft.

Tom looked her over again. "I'll take the couch."

"Can you feed the fish, too?"

Tom glanced back toward the living room. He didn't remember a fish tank. "Sure, I'll feed the fish." *If there were fish.* "Do you want help getting into bed?"

"I'll do it," she said.

"If you need anything, just holler," Tom said.

A trace of a smile came across Brynn's face, and she asked, "You still trying to hook up with me?"

Tom chuckled, shook his head, and said, "Always."

She grinned, but then grimaced when she shifted her weight.

"I'll be on the couch if you need me," Tom said.

"Tom?"

Tom paused, with his hand on the door handle.

"Go feed the fish, and come sit for a while," she said.

"I thought you said we'd sleep," Tom said.

"Go feed them and come back. I just want to talk a bit," she said.

Tom hesitated, and then went into the living room, found the small fish tank, and sprinkled a bit of the food across the surface of the water. Three fish made their way upward to meet it. He went to the kitchen, applied hand-sanitizer and rubbed it in, feeling the alcohol sting. He returned to her bedroom, and found her beneath the covers. He moved to the side of the bed and carefully sat.

She took a deep breath. She looked vulnerable, more child than woman.

"I'm going to die and I never accomplished a fucking thing," she said.

"You don't have to die," Tom said.

She smiled. "I'm not wired right. I can't last too much longer. I jumped off a balcony today."

"I know, I was there."

"We've both known people like me. So impulsive, so sensitive to everything, so wounded," she said.

She'd clearly spent time thinking about this. *Was this speech rehearsed? Was it honest? Was there an ulterior motive?*

"I'm sure you've accomplished things in your life," Tom said. It wasn't that he was trying to make her feel at peace with dying, but he didn't know what else to offer.

"I really haven't. Not even the normal stuff. I'll never have kids, or even a husband. I'll never own my own house. I'll never have a career," she said.

"You're not even thirty years old yet, you have time," Tom said.

"That's bullshit," she said.

"Brynn, people reinvent themselves in their sixties; it's not too late. You can do whatever you want," Tom said.

"Anything?" she asked.

Tom smiled.

"Okay, Tom, I want to go to an ivy-league school," she said.

His smile fell.

She said, "I want to get a job working as a spy, with a top-secret security clearance. I want to be a spy working for Chad."

"Who is Chad?" Tom asked.

"The Republic of Chad, dummy. The country, in Africa," she said.

Tom said, "Well, I can't do that either."

"I want to be the first female player in the NBA," she said. "You said I could do whatever I want."

"So, okay, you're right. Some things might be out of reach," Tom said.

"So where is that line, huh? How far does my reach go? Because right now it feels like I can't live another week, and I haven't done fuck-all with my waking-nightmare of a life," she said.

Tom wasn't sure what to say. Highlight the positive? She'd only take it as his invalidating her feelings, as being patronizing, or as a sign that he didn't understand. Worst of all, she was, to some extent, right. She didn't have a fresh start, a clean slate. Whatever she did going forward, she would be followed by her past, just as everyone is. Still, Tom didn't really understand what was so terrible about her life. She had a decent apartment; apparently some money was coming from somewhere.

"Don't think about what you haven't accomplished. Don't say you're not strong enough to make it to next week. Make it to tomorrow," Tom said, knowing how lame that sounded.

"Why?" she asked.

"If for no other reason, out of curiosity," Tom said. "I have no way of promising things will get better. I have no idea. But can't you be just a bit curious?"

"Curious about what?"

"I don't know. 'Will Tom be here in the morning? Does he really want to hook up with me, or is that just some bullshit I say when I try to be funny or to shock him?'"

She smiled. "You want me to be curious about *you*?"

Tom smiled back. "Why not?"

"You're too boring," she said, laughing, but then winced again.

Tom said, "Why don't you collect your story, the wisdom you've gained from living life the hard way."

She suddenly looked unsure, maybe hurt.

"I'm not blaming you. I don't know enough about you to guess. But I'm also guessing your life wasn't happy and easy, and then suddenly, you found yourself here," Tom said.

She nodded.

"Why don't you write that story?" Tom asked.

She was quiet a moment, and then asked, "Can you write it?"

"You should write it," Tom said.

She turned her head away. "Whatever."

Tom watched as she took a deep breath and let it out slowly. *Was he being manipulated? Was he too cynical? Maybe he should write her story.*

"Tell me something about you. Something from your past," Tom said.

"I was raped," she said.

Tom thought maybe she had been, or some sort of assault. It always seemed that these types of women...

"See, that's what I'm afraid of," she said.

"What?" Tom asked.

"I was never raped, but when I said that, you got a total like 'I fucking knew it' look on your face," she said.

Shit. This kid was too perceptive. Sensitive, she'd called it. Unfortunately, these amazing powers of insight often led to massive leaps to conclusions, if not leaps from balconies, about the motives of others, which caused cynicism at least and, at worst, paranoia.

"Nothing traumatic like that happened, OK? There was no pivotal moment in my life that explains why I'm this fucked up now. I had a nice childhood, and a nice family. We didn't have much, but I was loved, OK? And I was told I was smart and pretty. I had a few friends, I wasn't picked on or bullied, and I got decent grades. I even played soccer in 9th grade, and had three nice boyfriends in high school. I drank a bit, smoked a little grass, but nothing like Ben smokes, and he's all fucking zen and shit," she said.

Tom just stared back, not knowing what to say.

"Maybe I should smoke more dope?" she asked.

Tom said, "Maybe you should just get some sleep. We can talk more tomorrow."

"Why tomorrow?" she asked.

"Why not tomorrow? You're exhausted, I'm exhausted. And your life will still be fucked up tomorrow," Tom said. "We can pick this back up then."

"Whatev," she said.

"Night, Brynn," Tom said.

He rose. She closed her eyes, smiled, and pursed her lips for a kiss goodnight. He smiled as well and tapped her lips lightly with his fingertips. Her eyes shot open and then she licked her lips, grimacing. "Ugh. Hand sanitizer."

Tom laughed. "Goodnight." He walked into the living room, glanced once over at the fish tank, and then lay down on the couch. He tried to sleep but tossed and turned most of the night. Brynn was only fifteen feet away.

<u>8</u>

Allan walked in and, before he could even sit at his desk, Tom ran the idea by him.

"Instead of the little features on every tenant, I want to write an in-depth piece on a single tenant, maybe even a series. She lives upstairs, she's complex, interesting, and disturbed. There's a legit story there," Tom said.

Allan said, "Doesn't sound like refrigerator news."

Tom winced. "It isn't, but I'm going to write it."

Allan paused, pulled his chair closer to his desk, and then said, "Be careful. I know you're not brand new to this, but listen. There was this kid once, a teacher's kid, real weirdo. Not strange in the cliché creative artistic kid sense; he was just really off. He once appeared in the paper because he helped save a young girl from drowning. It was his fifteen minutes, you know? Made him much worse. Later in life, he bought a navy uniform and marched with medals in the parades. He couldn't drive a car, but he had a bicycle that he'd tow a little cart with. All around the town, he towed that cart filled with cheap trophies. Trying to reclaim that moment, that feeling of being special. He didn't live to be forty years old."

"How many of these kids are cutting themselves because they think no one sees them, no one cares?" Tom asked.

"I don't think that's why they cut," Allan said.

"I could potentially reach a bunch of young people just like her," Tom said.

"Are there a bunch? You might actually create a bunch with a story about her," Allan said.

Dennis appeared and asked, "Story about who?"

Tom wasn't prepared to sell it yet, especially in light of Allan's concerns. "There's this young woman, who lives above me."

"Oh, so, one of your features?" Dennis asked.

"She was originally, but I want to set that aside and go deeper on this story. There's more here," Tom said.

"More, how?"

"Well, she's self-destructive, and has attempted suicide multiple times. She believes her life has been a total waste of potential and that she's accomplished nothing," Tom said.

"Has she accomplished nothing?" Dennis asked. "If so, there's not much of a story."

Tom was surprised that Dennis was asking questions instead of issuing an immediate order to drop the story on Brynn. He said, "She's smart and can provide insight into her mental illness. It would be a feature on the hidden suffering of some of these young people in Portage."

"Is she from Portage? Or is she from away?"

"She lives in Portage now," Tom said. "I don't know if she grew up here."

"That makes a difference, don't you think?" Dennis asked.

"How?"

"Well, if she's from Massachusetts, then it's one more story of the flatties sending their problems north while moving in and buying up property," Dennis said.

Tom sank in his seat a bit.

"If she grew up here, then the problem is more serious," Dennis said. "However, either way, I'm not sure it's refrigerator news. The story you wrote about Marie, the UFO lady, that was fine, but this…"

Allan's eyebrows rose in a silent *I-told-you-so*.

"Why don't I take a first pass at it and see where it goes?" Tom asked.

Dennis paced a bit, seemingly thinking it over. Tom could write the story no matter what Dennis thought, but he wanted the piece to run in the paper, and it was Dennis who would decide that.

Allan drew a breath as if to say something, but then Dennis stopped pacing and said, "Well, write it and let's see. And if she's from away, I'll tell you right up front, I'm less interested. Oh, and don't set the other stories aside. Let's continue with a feature on each of the other tenants, just as we had planned. You'll have to write your longer piece concurrently and her story will run last, assuming we can use it at all."

Tom was surprised, and Allan looked confused. Dennis didn't say anything more; he just walked away.

Allan said, "Now you actually have to write it *while* writing the others, not to mention any actual news that comes in."

9

When Tom went onto the balcony the next day, Ben was there, smoking a joint.

"You don't worry about getting caught with that out here?" Tom asked.

"Wow, you look exhausted, you okay? And caught by who?" Ben asked.

He was right. What cop in his right mind would care about one guy with one joint?

"I'm going to write a longer story about Brynn," Tom said, looking up, wondering if she was right above them, listening.

"Want to walk and talk?" Ben asked.

"Let's just go down the street," Tom said.

As they reached the bottom of the stairs, Miguel came by on his unicycle. "Hey guys," he said.

"What's up," Ben said, and Tom nodded.

Miguel fell backward onto his running feet, and caught the moving unicycle by the seat. "Not much. Just chillin'. You know, man."

"I hear ya," Ben said.

"Is he cool?" Miguel asked Ben.

Ben raised the half-smoked joint in his hand.

"Oh good, man, I thought I smelled it but never know what

I'm really sensing, you know?" Miguel said. "So, can you hook me up?"

"How much?"

"I got like forty bucks, man," Miguel said.

Ben said, "I'll come by later. Will you be home?"

Miguel grinned. "Where else would I be, man?"

"I gotta go to work later. I'll swing by before I go," Ben said.

"Right on," Miguel said, and in one deft move, he was atop his unicycle again, pedaling toward apartment 1A.

"Do you supply pot to the whole building?" Tom asked.

Ben ignored the question and asked, "What about the story on Brynn?"

Tom shrugged, and said, "I'm writing a longer feature, more in-depth, on Brynn. You know, a look at why she cuts, why she jumps, etc. She told me last night that she was never a victim of abuse or anything, so there's no cliché standing by, ready to be used as an explanation for her behavior. She told me she had a very nice childhood." Tom said.

Ben said, "So it's confusing to you that she cuts and tries to kill herself."

They walked to the sidewalk and slowly strolled.

"Why does she do that?" Tom asked.

"Did she tell you why?"

Tom said, "She feels like she hasn't done anything with her life and she feels like she has little time left and, even if it's suicide, it's all out of her hands."

"I agree that most of the time suicide is something that happens to people more than it is something they choose for themselves," Ben said. "I think it's shitty when we say someone 'committed' suicide, makes them sound like a criminal or something. Like, we could say she was a victim of suicide."

"She seems pretty sure it can't be prevented," Tom said.

"She wants you to get her story down, so no matter what happens to her, she'll live on?" Ben asked. "Isn't that dangerous? I mean, as soon as you finish writing your story and it's published, won't that be a green light for her to kill herself?"

"She attempts it on a regular basis now," Tom said.

Ben said, "She might get better at it, with less room for error, or less luck."

Just then, Mr. Hitch went by on rollerblades. He was wearing two t-shirts, navy over white, and a pair of Adidas running pants. His belly strained against the shirts. On his head were oversized headphones, with strands of grey hair blowing about. Tom thought he heard Neil Diamond singing "Beautiful Noise" as Hitch skated by. Both Ben and Tom stared for a moment.

Turning back to Ben, Tom asked, "So, do I not write it? I have to write some story about her. I mean, what would she think if I wrote about everyone but her?"

"It's a conundrum," Ben said.

Tom paused, thinking, and then asked, "Oh, do you know if she's originally from Portage?"

Ben said, "Born and raised here, man. Brynn's a native."

Just then, a small RV, or perhaps more a large van, came rolling into the parking lot. Across its nose was scrawled "Rialta" in a sweeping script. The vehicle was typical Winnebago white, with a low brick-red stripe. An older couple slowly climbed out and joined each other near the front bumper.

"The Kapels. Rich and Becky. They live in 3A. Retired and mostly nomadic," Ben said.

Tom looked up at apartment 3A, and asked, "But there are cats living up there, right?"

"Three of them. Brynn feeds them, and changes their box

from time to time," Ben said.

It made sense, since Brynn was right next door. Tom glanced at 3C farther down the balcony. "So, Mr. Hitch doesn't help with the cats?"

Ben raised his eyebrows but said nothing.

"Hi Ben," Becky Kapel called, waving emphatically with both hands, grinning.

"Is she simple?" Tom whispered.

"Becky. Rich," Ben said. "This is Tom, he's in 2B."

Rich and Becky changed direction and approached Tom directly.

"Rich Kapel. My wife, Becky," Rich said, extending his hand. He was tall, thin, with a deeply lined face. His wife had a warm face, but with blank eyes. Her hair had the type of monochromaticity only possible with box dye and her hips were impossibly wide for her narrow ribs. Tom shook Rich's hand and smiled at both of them.

"Are you saved?" she asked Tom. Ben rolled his eyes.

"I hope so," Tom said.

"Oh, there's no need to hope. When you have faith, you don't need hope or luck," Becky said. "Just take Jesus into your heart." Her smile was still that of the pleasantly drunk.

Ben said, "Faith, hope, luck. Personally, I'd like to have all three."

In the subsequent awkward pause, all of their smiles froze, until Rich said, "Let's go see the cats, honey."

"It was nice meeting you," Becky said. Tom thought he saw her give Ben a bit of an odd look, but with a nod from Rich, the two made their way to the stairs.

Tom and Ben watched the Kapels climb.

Tom said, "They seem nice enough."

Ben said, "Just enough."

Ben held up his joint, showing it was getting too short to hold by hand and thus signaling he needed to return to his apartment. Tom nodded his acknowledgment and Ben headed off.

Tom looked up to Brynn's apartment, and thought he should probably go check on her.

10

When Tom knocked on Brynn's door, he heard scurrying inside, and tried again.

"Brynn, it's Tom," he called through the closed door.

"Go away," Brynn said.

God, now what was she up to? He knocked again, although he was not sure why.

"Open the door, Brynn," Tom said.

"Please go the fuck away," Brynn said. The voice was matter-of-fact, not panicked or tearful or even distressed.

"I just want to make sure you're okay," Tom said.

"Go away!" she said, then she giggled and, to someone in the room with her, she said, "Don't stop, don't stop, he'll leave."

"What?" Tom asked.

"I'm serious, Tom! Go away!" Brynn said, and she giggled again.

"Is there someone in there with you?" Tom asked.

"For chrissakes, I'm getting laid OK? You remember sex, right?" Brynn asked. "Get away from my door. You're wrecking the mood."

This time, there was also a man's laughter. Tom didn't like that there was someone in there with her; he wasn't jealous, but she was so vulnerable, despite her threats.

"What, are you listening at the door now, you kinky freak?" she asked. She was openly laughing, and then she moaned.

Tom stepped back, hesitated only a moment, and then turned, nearly walking into Becky Kapel. She was shaking her head.

Becky said, "Hate the sin, but love the sinner, right?"

Actually, it was a sin he particularly liked; it was Becky's tone he hated. Without a word, Tom stepped around her and went downstairs to his own apartment. He decided writing Brynn's story could wait.

Once inside, he heard the two of them in the apartment above fall to the floor, probably from the couch. He stooped and pulled a bottle of Jameson's from a low cupboard and drank a swig of the Irish whiskey from the bottle. He was supposed to go into to work, and hadn't been in a few days, but he wouldn't go today either.

Tom sat with the bottle, opened the laptop, and spotted a folder on his desktop. It contained his novel. Opening the folder, he saw the icon representing that work, that document, the book that was going to someday be a bestseller. He selected it without opening it, and then dragged it to the trashcan on his desktop. Pausing, he took another swig of the whiskey. Years of work, sitting in the virtual trashcan, but still retrievable. He emptied the trashcan, and it was gone.

As the moaning upstairs grew louder, Tom began typing. It was chaotic, not structured at all like a newspaper story. It was an information dump, everything he could think of that had to do with Brynn: facts, thoughts, and questions. As he typed faster and faster, he could hear the rhythmic thumping upstairs, he could hear the moaning, and the giggling. He typed as loudly as he could, pounding on the keyboard while the noises upstairs built to their inevitable conclusion. Tom paused, and took another long draw on the whiskey, then he resumed writing.

11

Winnie suggested they go hiking and Tom agreed. When she came by his apartment, she was wearing a denim skirt with leggings beneath it.

"You're going to hike in a skirt?" Tom asked.

She laughed. "A lot of people do."

"Where should we go?" Tom asked. "I hear people like to hike Rattlesnake or Mt. Major."

"Ugh. All the flatties have found those places. The trails are packed, the roads are lined with parked cars. We'd have a more natural experience in Central Park," Winnie said.

"Why do so many people go there?" Tom asked.

She said, "Well, with Mt. Major, you get a big payoff with the view in exchange for precious little work. So, the minivans come up from Flattachusetts and Manch-vegas and wherever else, and they cram the trails full of their kids and ankle-biter dogs, and then they take selfies at the top to say they 'climbed a mountain today' on Twitter."

"Is it really that bad?" Tom asked.

"You can't even imagine. Local boys grew up climbing on the Rumney Rocks, and now the locals can't even get on them. Tourists come from all over; the rocks are so crowded these days that they look like sugar cubes covered in ants."

"Where should we go then?" Tom asked.

"I know a place where the locals go to hike," she said.

"What's it called?" Tom asked.

"I can't tell you. You're still too much of a flatty. You might tell the others," Winnie said, smiling broadly.

They drove for a while, and when they passed Mt. Major, Winnie was proven right. Both sides of the road were lined with cars, many with Massachusetts license plates. Tom looked up at the small, wooded mountain.

"All these people are stuffed into the woods on that little slope?" Tom asked.

"And they think they are getting out into the wild," Winnie said.

People milled about the cars, and Winnie had to slow down.

"A lot of their packs and gear look brand new," Tom said.

"Posers. We used to refer to stuff bought from EMS as Expensive Mountain Shit. We tend to buy our stuff secondhand," she said. "Look there."

Tom looked where she was pointing. A slightly overweight man, with a Manchester Fisher Cats ball cap, wearing a fleece jacket and knee-length cargo shorts was pulling what looked like ski poles from his trunk.

"$200 poles to walk up this little mountain while surrounded by 600 of your closest friends," Winnie said.

"That much?"

She said, "They can cost way more. I was being conservative."

"Why don't they just grab a stick off the ground?"

"I told you, because they're flatties and posers," Winnie said.

Tom looked out at them all with babies in carriers, and poles and packs. Only speaking to people in the their own little groups; all filled with desperation for distinction, en masse.

Tom and Winnie drove on until they turned into a small dirt road, and this they followed only a short way before parking. There were no other cars, and a trail disappeared into the saplings. Tall oak trees and pines stood all around them. Winnie walked around to the trunk of her car and pulled an old, weathered pack from it. This she handed to Tom, who shrugged it on. It was not very heavy.

"What's in it?"

She said, "Snacks, water, a blanket, matches, that kind of stuff."

They set off on the trail, with the remaining multicolored leaves brushing against their sleeves as he followed her through the tunnel of vegetation. The trail soon became steeper and they got into a rhythm. They spoke little, but Tom found himself smiling as he moved, as if the branches were scrubbing the outside world off. Winnie was ahead of him, and he watched her work her way, occasionally putting her hands on her own knees, pushing. She was too thin, Tom thought, but she was beautiful. The slope got steeper still, and Tom considered looking for a stick, but he didn't want to pause for fear of Winnie thinking he was tired. However, Winnie stopped only a few steps later and looked back the way they had come. Tom tried to hide how hard he was breathing, and Winnie noticed.

"Hey, it's not a macho thing, you know," Winnie said. "People who wrap their ego around summit busting, you know, getting to the top quickly, they're missing the whole point. They are missing all the zen, man."

"I know," Tom said, but he still wouldn't let himself just breathe. He was not trying to bust mountains, but he didn't want Winnie to think he was a complete mess either.

"People who want to climb for the workout, they should just buy a treadmill," Winnie said. "It's like they say, the ego climber rejects the 'here,' man, because he's so concerned with what's up there, but when he gets there, it becomes the new 'here' and so he fakes excitement at reaching the summit, and he's not enjoying the climb, not really. What he wants is all around him, but he rejects it because it is all around him."

Tom looked around. He *looked*. Not just trees, but light. Not just terrain, but moss on boulders and fallen logs. Sound, beyond his breathing, of birds and wind. The smell of browning ferns and newly-fallen leaves, pine, and earth.

"This is it, man," Winnie said. "This is what the posers are missing. They are *missing* it, right?"

"Right," Tom said.

They continued up the trail, and Tom was aware now, in such a different way. He breathed freely, he touched branches that just minutes before he would have ducked and dodged. He paid attention to the resistance of the surface beneath his boots. He didn't just see light; he also saw shadows.

When they reached the top, they looked out across Squam Lake, made famous by the movie *On Golden Pond*, and preserved by a local association. Dotted with islands and its many coves reaching into the forest all around it. A boat was lazily picking its way through the rocks hidden beneath its glassy surface.

"Amazing," Tom said.

"Enjoy the *here*, Tom," Winnie said and smiled.

Tom smiled back, said, "Thanks," and he tried to absorb it all.

12

The interview with the Lennox brothers, Mike and Matt, began late one evening.

"We're not gay, we just aren't really into the whole thing. Women. Dating, a ring, getting married, kids, all that shit. I mean, we get to keep our money, we don't tell each other what to do, there's never any guilt, no trying to guess what someone really wants or means, no one telling us what we really feel," Mike said. "Who needs it?"

Matt said, "Really, I think most people get married and have kids because others expect them to. It's on their list of things to do."

Tom asked, "So you don't think its possible for married couples to be happy?"

"Happy in what way?" Matt asked.

"A lot of them think they're happy, but then they wake up one day and they look around and think, 'How the hell did this happen?'" Mike said.

"I suppose some people are really happy," Matt said. "I just know I wouldn't be."

"The happiest marriages seem to be couples where the husband immediately does whatever the wife says, or at least doesn't fight anymore. Just gives up. It's either that or listen to the nagging and bitching and give in eventually anyway," Mike said.

"You don't seem to have high opinions of women in general," Tom said.

"Don't get us wrong," Matt said. "There are great women out there. I just think it costs a man a lot to live with most women. Men grow old and broken trying to make women happy, but some women don't know how to *be* happy."

"Or don't want to be happy. It's like they can't be happy unless they're proven right about how messed up the world is and how meaningless their lives are," Mike said.

Tom thought of Brynn and how she felt she had never accomplished anything. Certainly, she wasn't representative of the average woman. *Or was she? What about Winnie?*

"What about someone like Winnie?" Tom asked, but immediately regretted it. He adjusted the recorder on the coffee table, turning it, without any real reason.

Mike smiled, and asked, "What about her?"

"You're right," Matt said. "She seems like she's actually happy, but she lives alone and you have to admit she's weird. Maybe being happy automatically makes a woman weird."

Tom wanted to take this a different way. "Tell me about you guys. Tell me about work and what you do for fun."

"You know we hang sheetrock," Mike said.

"Where are you working right now?" Tom asked.

"A couple residential jobs; one in the Valley and one on Winnie. The lake, not the chick downstairs," Matt said, laughing. "Working for rich people from away."

"And we have a bakery coming up," Mike said.

"Got to have another bakery; the tourons need their scones," Matt said, and both brothers chuckled.

"Do you guys like anyone?" Tom asked.

The brothers looked at each other, apparently confused, and

then looked back at Tom.

"What do you mean?" Mike asked.

"You were hard on women, now you're slamming flatties and tourists," Tom said.

Mike said, "Whatever, man. You don't know what it's like. You live here your whole life, right? And then these people, these transplants, come up here, buy up the best land or maybe marry a local who inherited some, buy up the lake and dress like city-hipsters and buy rural farmland they can't possibly farm, and then they start pushing for laws that have never been here before. Like your dog's got to be on leash or you can't burn brush in your backyard. Next, they'll have us wearing helmets on our fucking motorcycles."

"You guys make me glad that I'm from New Hampshire," Tom said.

"I thought you came up from Hooksett," Matt said.

"Yeah. Hooksett, New Hampshire," Tom said.

"Hooksett ain't New Hampshire, man. Everything south of Concord is just northern Massachusetts," Mike said, and both of the brothers laughed again.

"And everything north of Concord is the real New Hampshire?" Tom asked.

"You got that right. Except for maybe the outlets down in Tilton," Mike said.

"And you two are true Granite Staters, doing your own thing, when all these outsiders come up here, drive up the price of land on Squam, and start changing the laws?" Tom asked.

Matt said, "Fucking right. Live free or die, man. State motto and all that? Apparently, these Mass-holes can't read. It's on every license plate, for fucksakes."

License plates stamped out in prisons. This interview was going sideways. Tom asked, "Okay, so what do you do for fun?"

The brothers shared another look, but this one was furtive and nervous.

Tom asked, "What?"

Mike said, "Nothing, man. We don't have much time for fun. We work. We watch a DVD or whatever. In the fall, we like to hunt."

Matt said, "We fish sometimes."

"The other night, when I got back from the hospital with Brynn, what were you guys loading into the back of your truck? What was that about?" Tom asked.

"It was just work stuff," Matt said quietly.

"Why do you want to know?" Mike asked.

Tom knew he had stumbled onto something they didn't want to talk about. *Maybe it was drugs? A meth lab, possibly?* If so, he should back off, but he didn't really want to; perhaps it was his resentment of being limited to refrigerator news. Tom didn't really give a shit about what had been in the truck. He considered pushing further, but then decided against it. He'd already seen one neighbor jump from a balcony. *Why press this?*

"Just doing my job," Tom said. "You don't have to answer anything you don't want to."

"It was just work stuff," Matt said again.

Mike leaned forward. "Off the record?"

Tom regretted the whole thing now. He didn't want to know, and yet, he reached out and turned off the recorder.

"Off the record," Tom said.

"I dunno," Matt said.

Mike looked at his brother for a minute before saying, "We blow shit up."

Tom was confused, and searched both of their faces. "What

do you mean? With explosives?" Tom said.

Matt walked into the kitchen.

Mike said, "It's a real rush, you know?"

"Dynamite or what?" Tom asked.

"We don't have a license to buy that stuff, besides you can't just play with dynamite even if you have a license," Mike said.

"So what then?"

"We make stuff. Black powder, things like that," Mike said. "We go out to an old mica mine, up in the woods on this one hill."

Matt returned. "You can't tell anyone."

"It's off the record," Tom said.

"Not just that, you can't tell *anyone*. It's a pretty serious crime," Matt said, clearly worried.

"You do it just for kicks? You don't plan to blow your way into a bank or anything, right?" Tom asked.

Both brothers laughed, but the tension in the room was unalleviated.

"No, man, we're not going to become terrorists. Our jobs are pretty boring, you know? Plus, I figure that we're always constructing something, so I think it's like a release or some shit to destroy something," Mike said.

"What do you destroy?" Tom asked.

"Sometimes we'll bring a junk car out there. Or furniture. Random shit," Matt said.

"Aren't you worried about being hurt?" Tom asked.

"The danger is part of it. We're always nervous, and every time we blow something up, we laugh," Mike said.

"Like that nervous laugh, you know? Like giggling," Matt said.

"How long have you been doing this?" Tom asked.

"Years, man, like I don't even know," Matt said, looking to Mike for help.

"Yeah, years," Mike said.

"You don't store that stuff here, do you?" Tom asked, scanning the apartment.

The brothers looked at each other, and Mike said, "We don't really want to get into all that."

"If you're worried about us blowing up the building, you can stop worrying," Matt said. His smile was wide and reassuring, but it didn't really help.

An awkward silence fell, and the three men just looked at each other.

"So, anything else you want to tell me about you, Portage, or whatever?" Tom asked, snapping the recorder back on.

"Yeah, tell the college they should pay some of the local taxes. They keep buying houses from taxpayers, and we have fewer and fewer properties being taxed, so they're screwing things up for the rest of us," Mike said.

"But you guys rent," Tom said.

"Yeah, Mike, we rent, man. We don't pay property tax," Matt said.

"Whatever, they get us in other ways," Mike said.

There was another brief silence. "I think I have enough," Tom said, picked up the recorder, and turned it off. "Thanks, guys."

"No sweat," Mike said.

"Don't say nothing about that off-the-record stuff," Matt said.

"I won't," Tom said. What could he say or even write anyway? The time would probably be better spent filling sandbags to line the wall between his apartment and theirs.

He left their apartment, and at the far end of the balcony sat Miguel. His unicycle was at the bottom of the stairs, leaning against the railing. Tom approached and saw his ear buds were in and he was reading, and then Miguel noticed him.

"Hey man," he said, pulling the buds from his ears.

"Hey Miguel," Tom said. "Everything okay?"

"Oh, just fine, man. Just like the sun on my face. One downside of living on the ground is that I have no balcony like this," Miguel said. "Nice to get an aerial view on life now and then."

"Can I ask you something?" Tom asked.

"Do it," Miguel said.

"How'd you end up in Portage?" Tom asked.

"You mean because of my ethnicity?"

"Mexican-American?" Tom asked.

"My people are from Venezuela, man, but I've been in Portage since 5th grade," Miguel said.

"How was the transition for you?" Tom asked, moving to Miguel's right and sitting beside him.

"At first it was rough, right?" Miguel said. "I mean, the locals thought we were Puerto Ricans, and they were hostile. Like, not overtly, you know, but it was there."

"What changed?" Tom asked.

"I can run, man. Or I used to be able to," Miguel said. He grinned. "I'm like forty now, and I smoke and all, but when I was a kid, I was super fast."

"So, the locals warmed to you because you could run?" Tom asked.

"Yeah, man, like if you can do something special, it gives them all a 'but.'"

"A 'but?'" Tom asked.

"Dude, like, 'Yeah, he's a Puerto Rican, *but* he can run, and the track team could sure use him," Miguel said.

Tom was quiet for a moment, and then asked, "Can you speak Spanish?"

"Some, you know, but I'm rusty. Friggin' Ben speaks it better than me. I wish my family was still around; they'd have loved to practice with him. He's always after me, like, asking me what's the Spanish past-participle for *cocinar* or some shit like that," Miguel said.

"What is the past-participle for *cocinar*?" Tom asked.

Miguel smiled. "It's *cocinado*, dude, but I had to, like, look it up. I mean, I didn't even know what a participle was, you know?"

"What language do the voices speak?" Tom asked.

"One is a man who speaks English, and there's a woman who speaks Spanglish, and then there's a minor cast of others. None of them are hardcore Spanish speakers, maybe because even in my subconscious, I don't have enough left to draw on," Miguel said.

"Some people think everything you've ever heard, seen, or read is still stored in your head, but 'forgetting' just means you can't seem to access the memory that's there," Tom said.

Miguel seemed to consider this for a moment and then said, "In my case, I have more than one person using these memories. If what you say is true, what if some of the voices in my head can remember things I can't?"

"That'd be scary," Tom said.

"Right on, man. Like, I could blackmail myself or something, like a voice could say 'Do this or that, or else I'll unleash a truly horrible memory on your ass,'" he said, and laughed.

Tom looked out toward the horizon and asked, "Where's your family now?"

"They moved. A bunch of them live in Boston. Jamaica Plain. A couple live in Manchester," Miguel said.

"You stay in touch?" Tom asked.

Miguel shrugged. "Hey are you interviewing me right now?"

"Completely off the record," Tom said.

"Hey man, you must read, right? Like, all writers read, right?" Miguel asked.

"I think that's true," Tom said. "Except for Snooki."

"Huh?" Miguel asked, handing him the manuscript he had been reading. It was an unbound half-ream of paper, the top sheets wrinkled and a bit dirty.

"Never mind. What is it?" Tom asked, taking it. The title read, "Tupac Was the Buddha."

"Something to think about," Miguel said.

"You wrote this?" Tom asked.

"Whoa, no way, man," Miguel said. "But I dig it."

"Is it a self-help book?" Tom asked, flipping through it.

Miguel nodded, and said, "Something like that." He looked off into space, and Tom looked that way, too, but couldn't see what had Miguel's attention, and then he just put his ear buds back in. Conversation over. Tom stood, and walked back to his apartment.

13

Tom sat in his apartment, with the television off, writing. It was a story in which he'd have to leave out the most interesting part.

> The brothers Lennox hang sheetrock for a living, and have had a ringside seat while their community has been transformed by newcomers to the region.
> Mike, 24, and his brother Matt, 26, worry that people from away have purchased much of the most desirable real estate in the area.

Someone knocked once, and then again.

Tom asked, "What?" *Weird. Who knocks and then waits to enter?*

"Can I come in?"

It was Allan's voice. He hadn't been to the office in five days, and so, now it had come to him.

"It's open," Tom said.

Allan entered, dressed in khakis, polo shirt, and a light jacket. He glanced around the room while Tom walked over, picked a shirt up off the living room floor, and walked into the bathroom. He tossed the shirt into the hamper.

From the other room, Tom heard Allan say, "We're kind of

wondering what happened to you. Haven't seen you in a while."

"Working from home," Tom said as he returned. The two men stood facing each other, and Tom brushed down a bit of unruly hair with the palm of his hand.

"Are you?" Allan asked.

Tom moved to his laptop, and lifted it so that Allan could see that he had been writing the piece on the Lennox brothers.

"So you are," Allan said. "You know, you're still expected to come into the office now and then."

"Yeah, I know, I was planning to go in today, in just a little bit," Tom said.

"It's Sunday," Allan said.

"Yeah, I know, just thought I'd go," Tom said. *Why was Allan here?*

They remained standing, still facing each other. There was a moment of silence before Allan said, "I'm worried about you. You look really tired."

"Don't worry," Tom said.

"Dennis is worried, too," Allan said.

Ah, there it is. "He doesn't need to be."

Allan walked over to a chair, pulled a Red Sox hat off the seat, tossed it onto the pile of paper on the coffee table, sat, and waited. Tom sighed and went to the couch.

"Did he send you to fire me?" Tom asked.

"I came to see if you had quit without telling us," Allan said.

Tom said, "I know I have to go in more often."

Allan said, "Every day."

"What?"

Allan said, "He wants you to come in every day, at least for a while. You know, to prove you still work there."

"But I was always going to work from home a couple days a week," Tom said.

Allan leaned forward and glanced around the room, and asked, "What's happening to you?"

"Nothing. I've been writing from home, that's all," Tom said.

There was no knock; the door simply opened, and then Winnie poked her head in.

"Bad time?" she asked.

"Come on in," Tom said.

"We're just talking about work. I'm Allan Morrison. I work with Tom at the paper."

"Winnie Millen."

"You work at the bookstore, right?" Allan asked.

"Well, now that we all know where we work..." Tom said.

Allan stood, and said, "Here, Winnie, sit here. I'm leaving. Tom, see you tomorrow."

Tom didn't stand or respond.

"Nice meeting you," Allan said.

"You, too," Winnie said.

Allan left, careful with the door as he closed it. Winnie moved beside Tom on the couch, and asked, "Are you okay?"

Tom stood, and said, "I have to go to work tomorrow."

"Sounds like a good idea," Winnie said.

"This place is actually starting to feel like home," he said.

"And that's a good thing?"

"You live here," Tom said.

"I *sleep* here," Winnie said.

"Whatever, these people are growing on me," Tom said.

"You've got a chance coming up to see the entire herd in one place," she said.

"What do you mean?" Tom asked.

"The annual cookout. Next week. I just saw a flier on the post outside my apartment," she said.

"What should I bring?" Tom asked.

"Just what you'll eat. There are always extras, too."

"Tofu, then," he said.

"Fuck off," she said, smiling.

"Does everyone attend?" Tom asked.

"Everyone came last year, except for Mr. Hitch."

"What's his story, anyway?"

"I was hoping to read his story once you've finished writing it," she said.

"Seriously," Tom said.

"I don't know. He was here when I got here. He keeps to himself, wears strange stuff, rarely talks to anyone."

Tom paused, and was taken with how pretty Winnie was in her simple grey t-shirt, jeans, and flip-flops. He reached out and touched her hair, and she didn't move. They kissed, and he pulled her close. She brought her hands up between them, smiled, and pushed him away.

"What's wrong?" Tom asked.

"That's enough for now," she said. "Take a shower, go put in a full day's work tomorrow, and then come find me."

Tom smiled, and said, "I thought you were all Earth-mother, you know, like, a couple days without a shower would turn you on."

"I think it's been more than a couple days."

"Ouch!" Tom said, laughing. "C'mon. Even Brynn is getting some lovin'."

She laughed, and said, "Feel free to go see if Mike will sleep with you, too, then."

"She slept with Mike? That was *Mike*?" Tom asked.

Winnie laughed again. "Come find me after work tomorrow," she said, "and keep the 7th open."

"What for?"

"For the cookout, next week," she said.

"Oh, right," he said.

After she left, Tom sniffed one armpit. She was right. He may have to burn this shirt.

* * *

Later that afternoon, Tom found a cat on the balcony just outside his door. It had a beautiful coat but was morbidly obese. He then heard Becky, one floor up.

"Lassiter. C'mon kitty. C'mon Lassiter."

Tom asked the cat, "You're name is Lassiter?"

"C'mon kitty," Becky continued to call.

"Becky, he's down here I think," Tom said.

Becky's face appeared as she looked down to confirm it was her cat.

"Oh!" Becky said. "What's he doing down there?"

Many smart-assed answers flooded simultaneously into Tom's head, but he decided to play nice. "Just hanging out with me," Tom said.

"Well, he's an indoor kitty," Becky said. "Would you mind bringing him up to me?"

Fuck. "No problem," Tom said, scooping up the cat. It went limp, and felt like a twenty-pound bag of birdseed wearing a fur coat. Becky took the thing in a two-armed hug.

"Thank you so much," she said.

"Interesting name," Tom said.

"Yes, our little Lassie has quite a name, doesn't he?" she said, nuzzling the cat, who seemed to hardly notice the woman as she held him.

"You realize you named a cat Lassie?" Tom asked.

She just blinked at him with a dull smile.

"You know, like the dog. Lassie. Like 'Timmy fell down a well' Lassie," Tom said.

Becky smiled a bit more broadly but said nothing, and Rich stepped out then.

"What's he doing outside?" Rich asked.

"He went for a little stroll," Becky said.

"Too bad he didn't find the street," Rich said.

What a dick. Tom needed to extract himself from this before he took his turn leaping over the railing. As he turned to go, Rich grabbed his arm.

"Come on in, Mr. Journalist. Come have a cup of coffee," Rich said.

"I really have to go," Tom said.

"Nonsense, come on in and have some coffee with us. The least we can do, after you brought Lassiter back to us," Becky said.

"Yeah, thanks a ton for *that*," Rich said. "Besides, you can start interviewing us."

"Well, I don't have my recorder or anything," Tom said.

"Oh, I wouldn't speak into one of those things for a million bucks. Editors can twist your words all around before they air them," Rich said.

"It's a newspaper," Tom said.

"I mean, look what they did to that nice detective," Becky said.

"Which?" Tom asked.

"That Detective Furman, at the O.J. Simpson trial," Becky said.

Did she really just say that?

"Twisted his words all around, tried to make him look like a monster," Rich said.

Tried? He was a crooked, racist cop suspected of planting evidence on a guy who was probably guilty to start with, thereby getting O.J. acquitted. Still, all Tom actually said was, "I see."

They stepped inside. The furniture was spare, with a crucifix on one wall and a framed quote on another. It read, "Faith is when you close your eyes and open your heart." Two more cats ran into the kitchen from the hallway.

"How do you take it?" Rich asked.

"Just a little sugar," Tom said.

Rich handed him a coffee, and they all sat around the small table. "So tell us about yourself?"

Oh no. "As you know, I'm a reporter at the paper. I've been doing that for a few years, at another paper before coming here. No serious relationships, my parents still live in Hooksett," Tom said. "I have no pets."

"Want three cats?" Rich asked.

"Oh, Rich," Becky said. "He acts like he doesn't like the cats, but he loves them."

"I don't," Rich said.

"Oh, you know you do," Becky said.

"Remember, scripture says not to dispute your husband," Rich said.

Becky waved him off and chased one of the cats off the countertop.

"I asked you once before, Tom," Becky said. "Are you saved?"

"Well, I've been baptized," Tom said.

Becky's face brightened. Rich took a sip of coffee.

"That's great!" Becky said. "What's your date?"

"My what?" Tom asked.

"The date. The day you accepted Jesus Christ as your personal savior," Becky said.

Tom sipped his coffee. *Horrible. Probably just enough coffee to make the water brown.* "I was baptized very young, I don't remember it."

Becky's face changed, almost to an expression of fear, and she whispered, "You're not a Catholic are you?"

Tom looked at Rich, whose face contained no clues at all as to his feelings on the subject, which Tom decided was information enough. "Not anymore."

Becky said, "Thank the Lord."

Rich took another sip, and so did Tom. Becky just stared with that blank smile. The silence was brutal.

"Yup," Tom said.

Rich suddenly spoke up, "You're not one of those journalists pushing the left-wing agenda, are you?"

"I wouldn't know what that agenda is," Tom said. Taking another sip, he figured the sooner he finished the coffee, the sooner he could leave.

"You know, like promoting things like evolution, abortion, and the gays," Rich said.

Okay, so, manners or not, Tom wasn't going to sit through much more of this.

"We've even had a Muslim president," Becky added.

Rich said, "Becky, don't start with that again. She'll go on and on about it, and I'm just sick of it. It doesn't matter what god, the damage to the country was done and can't be undone."

Becky said, "We're preparing for the end times. We've been stashing food, medicine, and even cigarettes. We have a place…"

Rich interrupted. "Jesus, Becky, shut up. Don't tell him all that. He doesn't need to know."

"Oh, right," Becky said. "Sorry."

"Women, right?" Rich said. "Be dangerous if they had brains."

Okay, all done. Tom couldn't take anymore.

"I'm sorry, but I really have to run. Thank you for the coffee," Tom said.

Becky rose, but Rich just took another sip.

"Come back again sometime. We can do that interview," Becky said.

"But no recorders," Rich said.

Tom found his way out, since neither of them followed him to the door.

14

That night, as Tom lay in bed, he reached down to the floor and lifted the manuscript to his chest. "Tupac Was the Buddha," Tom read aloud. No author listed. The manuscript was printed on three-hole paper, with a brass brad fastener in the top hole. Tom flipped a couple blank pages and then read:

PROLOGUE

Squeezed between the Baby Boomers and the Millennials are Generation X, born between 1962 and 1982, with only 50 million members. The Boomers who came before us number nearly 80 million, and there are approximately 95 million members of the Millennial generation who followed.

As a generation, we didn't have a mass ideological cathartic moment when we decided we should replace our leaders. There was no mass subscription to a single, abstract cause. Because of this, the Boomers misunderstood us, and could not label us. It was they who christened us "Generation X," a generation which could not be named. They thought this a criticism of a generation that, to them, didn't seem to care about anything. This, of course, was not true.

* * *

When we were kids, we watched a transformation. My family's home and the homes of all my friends, save one, were nearly identical. Two parents, a sibling or two, a lawn, a car and an old pickup truck. Our mothers stayed home even when we didn't, and we came home to them.

Divorces seemed to come with the arrival of disco in our preteen years, and they were contagious. Even in the homes that didn't break, once the oldest of us began driving our younger brothers and sisters to ballgames and movies, our mothers went to work. Generation X was the proto-latch-key kids. Our parents worried, but we found freedom. We became more independent and responsible. We took pride in being self-sufficient and in being able to work out problems for ourselves.

I would come home to an empty house and revel in the silence of it, in the space of it. In the beginning, I would do all the forbidden things. I wore my sneakers in the house. I sat on the countertop. I ate upstairs in my bedroom. I made a frozen pizza at 4pm to ruin my appetite for the dinner my mother would make later. I watched porn from my dad's VHS collection while drinking a bottle of his Heineken. And then I didn't. After about a week of that, I stopped. I took off my sneakers, stayed off the countertop, ate a small snack in the kitchen, left the beer alone, and cut back on the porn.

I got more homework done than I did when Mom had been home. Eventually, I started making dinner for the family so it would be ready when my parents came home. I cleaned. My generation and I came into our own. We took the opportunity to grow up. We weren't infantilized by our parents. We were expected to, asked to, and wanted to grow up, and we did.

Still, throughout all this, our parents tried to give us hope and optimism. Theirs was a generation raised by survivors of global conflict and economic depression, and so the hippies who became our parents told us of a bright future if we were willing to work for it; we did, and it came.

Tom put the manuscript down. He would try to get some sleep. He was going to work in the morning.

15

The next day, Tom walked into the office with no small amount of dread, and he resented feeling that way. He found Allan at his desk.

"Morning," Allan said.

"Should I expect a scolding?" Tom asked.

"Just act like you've been coming in every day. He hates confrontation. Pretend nothing is wrong. Laugh at his jokes, agree with whatever he says. None of this really matters anyway," Allan said.

"If it doesn't matter, what the hell am I doing here?" Tom said.

"A paycheck. Welcome to adulthood."

"Actually, lately, I feel more like a teenager than I have in a long time," Tom said.

"Your behavior certainly reflects that," Allan said.

Dennis came strolling in between their desks just then. "Good morning."

"Morning," Allan said.

"Morning," Tom said. It was incredibly difficult to act normal; he wasn't sure he even remembered what "normal" meant.

"Tom, at a local annual fundraiser, the NHS work as ushers. I think it would be interesting to get their perspective on that event. It would be a lens that those who don't attend could use to learn about the event and the NHS," Dennis said.

Dennis was acting as if Tom had been showing up all along, just as Allan predicted. "What's the NHS?" Tom asked.

"The honor society at the high school. The National Honor Society. You know," Dennis said.

"What about the pieces I'm writing now?" Tom asked.

"You can put them aside for a bit. The event is a timely thing. Those folks will still be living in your building after the event is over," Dennis said.

The tension in the room had risen a bit. Tom was on thin ice and was asking too many questions, passively resisting. He had just started the longer story on Brynn, and he was still writing the piece on the Lennox brothers. He had to interview the Kapels before they returned to the road. He didn't want to abandon— even temporarily—those stories in order to get the adolescent perspective on a fundraising event.

Tom looked at Allan, but there would be no help coming from him. Dennis's face was expectant as a priest's. *Just take your penance.* What if he quit? Just walked out? *How would people read Brynn's story? What would Winnie think? Or Ben at McDonald's? Or the Lennox brothers hanging sheetrock? Was this job so terrible?*

Dennis cleared his throat, and asked, "Any questions?"

Allan gave half a shrug.

"How do I get in touch with the NHS kids?" Tom asked.

Dennis paused before reaching into his shirt pocket and producing a folded slip of paper with a phone number on it. "This is Ashley's cell phone number."

"Ashley?" Tom asked.

"My niece. She's a member of the NHS and she's a good place to start," Dennis said.

Ah, of course, his niece. "Thanks," Tom said.

"No problem," Dennis said, and walked away. Allan sat nodding his sympathetic approval.

Tom looked at the phone number once more, and tossed it onto his desk. It was going to be a long day. He didn't call Ashley that afternoon. Instead, he worked on the story about the brothers, and then he just surfed the Internet. Allan, however, spent the day typing, scribbling notes, and making phone calls. Tom remembered working like that for his previous employer, but it now seemed so foreign to him. He couldn't move forward with the story on Brynn; he had gotten as far as he could without interviewing her. He'd have to set up some time with her, and maybe he'd see her at the cookout.

* * *

Tom drove home, pulled into the parking lot, and looked up at his dark apartment. Winnie's place had a warm yellow glow coming through the sheers. Walking over to her door, he knocked. When she opened it, she was wearing only a bathrobe.

"Found you," he said.

She smiled, and asked, "How was work?"

Stepping in, he closed the door behind him and took her in his arms. He kissed the side of her head, then her ear, and then her neck. She sighed, and let her head fall back. He scooped her up in his arms and carried her to the bedroom.

"This doesn't actually work on women, does it?" she asked.

"I've never tried it before. I'll let you know in a couple of hours," he said.

"Ooh, aren't you the ambitious one?"

"I'm willing to try," he said.

They kissed as he gently laid her on the bed and sat beside

her. He untied her robe, and laid the belt open. Then he stood, removing his own clothing. She lay smiling, not moving, just watching. Tom slowly opened her robe, exposing her impossibly white skin. She pulled her arms from the sleeves, and Tom began kissing her neck again, her throat, and her chest. They made love, and it was as if they had been lovers for years, but in their desire and nervousness, they were also like teens groping and grabbing for each other in the dark. It was generous, passionate, and complete.

16

Tom left Winnie's apartment the next morning around 9:00 a.m. As he stepped out into the sunlight, he could see Rich working at what looked like a grill almost directly in front of Marie's apartment. Copious amounts of smoke were rising into the sky, and if Tom had left a window open, it would be drifting into Tom's apartment right now.

"A bit early in the morning for barbecue, isn't it?" Tom asked.

Rich looked over, and Tom could see the look of disapproval on the older man's face; exiting Winnie's apartment in the morning was a sure sign of a sin committed. Still, Rich didn't mention it and instead only said, "It isn't barbecue. It's a smoker."

"I can see that," Tom said as he moved closer.

Rich lowered his voice. "It's part of the preparations. We're smoking meat, and then we're able to can it or vacuum pack it. It might not last forever, but it'll last a good long time."

"Beef?" Tom asked. "Like, jerky?"

"Everything. Beef, pork, turkey. Even some fish," Rich said. "But smoked, not dehydrated. Though we're doing that, too."

"Can I ask you something?" Tom asked.

Rich looked up at him.

"If the whole thing went to hell…" Tom began.

"Not to *hell*," Rich said.

"Okay, if there *was* an Armageddon…" Tom began again.

"There won't be 'an' Armageddon, there will be just the one," Rich said.

"I don't know how to say it," Tom said, exasperated. "What do you call what you're preparing for?"

"We're preparing for *when it hits the fan*," Rich said, smiling grimly.

"Fine. When the shit hits the fan," Tom said, "I want to know why you'd want to live any longer."

Rich's smile fell and he just stared.

"I mean, if the whole world has hit the fan, why would you want to survive that? Besides simply surviving, what would be the point of you and Becky living on beyond that time?" Tom asked.

Rich squinted. "I don't get it."

Tom said, "I assume that the world after 'it' hits the fan will be terrible."

Rich said, "It will be. There will be famine and bands of marauders looking for food and basic medicines."

Tom said, "None of the comforts of life. No community, man reduced to animal."

"Exactly," Rich said.

"Wrath-of-God type stuff," Tom said.

"Praise the Lord, and His judgment cometh soon," Rich said.

Tom took a step closer. "So, why survive it? Why do you want to see any of that? Wouldn't it be better to simply die and get your everlasting reward?"

Rich stood for a moment without saying anything. He was clearly processing, and then he said, "It isn't for us to assume we'll live or die. The Lord's plan might include us living, and he's given us the wisdom and wherewithal to prepare, but imagine our shame if we didn't heed the warnings and read the signs. Imagine if we didn't prepare. We would find ourselves in the End Times, not ready, having squandered the opportunities the Lord has provided."

Not a bad answer. Tom was about to ask something else when Rich interrupted. Rich raised one hand and said, "If we prepare, but then the Lord takes us up in the Rapture, then someone else—maybe even you—can find our stash. But if the Lord's design has us staying here, then we will be able to survive, thanks to His grace and mercy."

"So, you'll share?" Tom asked.

"If we're gone, then people should divide our stockpile," Rich said.

"And if you're *not* gone?" Tom asked.

"Anyone tries to take this," Rich said, and gestured to the smoker, "I'll put one right between his eyes and two in the chest."

Tom believed him. The two men stared at each other for a moment.

"Have a good day," Tom said.

"You, too," Rich said.

Tom turned and walked away. Rich called after him. "Tom, it's not too late for you. You stop your sinning and take Jesus into your heart, and you can be saved, too."

From the stairs, Tom said, "I don't think that would work. I don't own a smoker."

Rich waved with his tongs, and Tom returned to his apartment.

17

Tom knocked on Winnie's door and waited. When it opened, Tom could see the puzzled look on her face.

"Why didn't you just come in?" she asked.

"My sister," Tom said. He entered, stepping past her.

"Your sister?"

"My sister Trisha is coming. She'll be here today," Tom said.

"Is that a good thing? Are you not close or something?" Winnie asked.

"Just the opposite, we're very close," Tom said.

"So what's the problem?"

"I'm not sure," Tom said.

"What do you mean?"

"I mean, she'll ask how work is going, how things are going," Tom said.

"And you're worried she'll judge you?"

"I'm worried she'll worry," Tom said.

Winnie smiled. "She should. I worry about you."

"Why?" Tom asked.

Winnie's smile fell. "C'mon, Tom. You're in the midst of a huge life transition. You're reinventing yourself, probably for the first time since puberty. I worry, you worry, and she'll likely worry."

"How can I keep her from worrying?" Tom asked. "Should I lie about work and whatever?"

"I think you should tell her the truth, and then tell her not to worry," Winnie said.

"Will that work?" Tom asked.

"Not a chance, but it's your best move," Winnie said.

Tom hesitated and then asked, "Would you like to meet her?"

"You want help?" Winnie asked, and smiled again.

Tom said nothing, he only stared.

"Okay, let's go out to eat, Thai Hut. They have vegan organic Thai on the menu," Winnie said. "Will she go for that?"

"I think so, she's pretty hip," Tom said.

"When does she get here?"

"Later today," Tom said. "Driving up from Sudbury."

"She might be too tired," Winnie said.

"No, let's get Thai, and then we can come back here. She's leaving tomorrow. Just an overnight," Tom said. "We'll come get you around 8pm?"

"That'd be fine," Winnie said.

There was an awkward moment before he kissed her quickly, and was out the door.

* * *

When his sister Trisha arrived, Tom was just getting off the phone with Ashley, the NHS student who was his point-of-contact for the fundraiser.

"So, do people wear, like, a jacket and tie for this?" Tom asked. He closed his eyes. How had it come to this? Asking a high school kid for fashion tips.

"People wear all sorts of things. Some men are in full-on suits, and there were men last year wearing jeans, and then everything in between," she said.

With Trisha's knock, Tom walked toward the door and wrapped up the call. "Okay, thanks. I'll see you then. I'll meet you at the check-in table, like you said. Bye."

He hung up, not waiting for Ashley's response. Tom pulled the door open and his sister Trish stood there with a huge grin. She all but hopped at Tom, wrapping her arms around him. She felt good. As if a large safety net had suddenly been spread beneath him. Tom squeezed her tight.

"It's good to see you," Tom said.

"It's so good to see you, too," Trish said.

With one arm still around her, Tom closed the door.

"Listen, we're going out for Thai," Tom said.

Trish said, "I just got here."

"We won't be out long. I want you to meet someone," Tom said.

"Ooh, a special someone?"

Tom said, "She's pretty cool. She's suggested an organic vegan Thai place, but I'm sure the food's good anyway."

"That sounds great," Trish said.

"So you're hungry?" Tom asked.

"I could eat a bushel of tofu," she said, and smiled. "What's her name?"

"Winnie," Tom said.

"Like the sound a horse makes?" Trish asked.

"Like the lake," Tom said.

"Did you find yourself a greenie weenie?" Trish asked.

Tom said, "I think you'll like her."

"Does she smell? Hairy armpits? The whole bit?" Trish asked, teasing.

"All of that and more, a real keeper," Tom said.

They sat for a bit and caught up, talking about nothing until Trish asked, "How's the new job?"

Tom shifted, "Well, I get paid to write. That's a good thing."

"Uh-oh. That doesn't sound good," Trish said.

Tom stood. "It's really time to get going. We still have to pick up Winnie."

"Does she live far?"

"Not at all. In fact, I wouldn't be surprised if she's overheard our conversation," Tom said.

They left Tom's apartment, went by Winnie's, and then walked to the restaurant. It was farther than Tom would normally have walked, but it was only half-again as far as the newspaper office.

"How have I not noticed this place?" Tom asked.

"Hidden in plain sight," Winnie said. Trish chuckled.

The three of them entered. It was dark and quiet, with the only customers one couple in a booth. Winnie waved at the hostess who never left her spot near the bar, but who waved back with a smile. Winnie led them to a far booth.

"This okay?" Winnie asked.

Before Tom could answer, Trish said, "This is great. What a nice place."

Tom suddenly felt like the boyfriend intruding on a girls' night out.

"And you haven't been here, Tom?" Trish asked.

Tom said, "No, Winnie's kept this place a secret until now."

Trish rolled her eyes. "A secret on Main Street."

"I know, right?" Winnie said.

A young man, likely a relative of the Thai family that owned and ran the place, appeared and filled their water. He then distributed menus, and told them that their server would be right with them.

"What do you recommend?" Trish asked.

"Are you a vegetarian?" Winnie asked.

"I'm willing to learn," Trish said, and both women laughed. Tom couldn't help but smile.

"Try the green curry. It's made with lemongrass, green chilies, galangal, lime leaves, coconut milk, and wheat gluten instead of meat," Winnie said. "I bet you will love it."

Trish closed her menu and said, "Sign me up!"

Tom glanced through the menu and picked what he wanted just in time for the waiter to arrive. He looked to Winnie, who then ordered meals for herself and Trish. Tom then said, "I'll take a B4."

Trish opened and quickly checked her menu. She found it. "B4 is California roll, Tom. That's not even Thai."

"And three Tsingtao's," Tom said.

The waiter collected their menus and left to put the order in.

"It's not even really Japanese either, but it's what I feel like having. And just to mix it up, I ordered Chinese beer," Tom said. "Besides, who are you to judge? You're replacing your meat with wheat gluten."

"It's good!" Winnie said.

"I thought gluten was one of the new things to be avoided at all costs," Tom said.

Trish shook her head, and Winnie giggled. Tom took a sip of his water. The waiter returned with three more glasses and three bottles of beer.

"Can a vegan drink this?" Trish asked.

"Yeah, usually the only thing that ruins beer for me is honey," Winnie said.

They poured, glasses were raised without a spoken toast, and each had a sip. Before Tom's glass was back on the table, Trish asked, "So, Tom, really, how's work going?"

Tom glanced at Winnie, and Trish picked up on it. "Oh-oh, what's wrong? Did you get fired?"

"I didn't get fired. I'm just having a bit of a tough time staying motivated to go into work and write 'refrigerator news,' you know, stories people post on the fridge," Tom said.

"Ugh. Is that what they call it?" Trish asked. "That does sound grim."

Tom said, "So, I'm plugging away at it, but in the next few days, I've got to cover a town council meeting…"

"Board of Selectpeople, actually," Winnie said.

Tom said, "…and a fundraiser where I'll follow some honor-student ushers around."

Trish sighed. "So you find yourself in the unique position of having to do stuff at work that you'd rather not do?"

Tom smiled. "That's it exactly." She always did distill these things down.

"Are you looking for work elsewhere?" Trish asked.

"I'm really not sure what I want to do," Tom said.

Trish said, "That doesn't sound like you."

"Well, I'm going through an adjustment of some sort, I think. I think I'm changing, maybe my eyes are opening," Tom said.

"What brought this change on?" Trish glanced at Winnie.

"I don't think it was me," Winnie said. "Not by myself, anyway."

"I'm not sure. I think some of it is just living with real people again, like when we were little kids. A place where people live with less than they thought they'd have, and yet most of them have maintained a sense of humor and held off bitterness somehow," Tom said.

"Interesting," Trish said.

The waiter returned, this time with their food.

"This looks great," Trish said.

"I hope you like it," Winnie said.

"So, how's your book coming?" Trish asked.

"I've shelved it. I feel like there's a bigger story to write. I'm not sure I've found it, but maybe. If not, I'll keep looking," Tom said.

"What bigger story?" Trish asked. "Like, for the newspaper, or another book?"

"I'm not sure yet," Tom said.

"Are you sure you're okay?" Trish asked.

"I don't want you to worry," Tom said. "I'm just looking for the next thing."

Trish took a bite. "I love it."

"I hoped you would," Winnie said, smiling.

18

The Selectboard of Portage, New Hampshire, met the 2nd and 4th Wednesday of every month. This meeting began with a review of the minutes from the last meeting, and approval without amendment. The members of the board then reviewed an application for a liquor license renewal, which they promptly signed without comment.

The chairperson, Virginia Yungster, owned and operated a local health food and vitamin supplement store. Outside of these meetings, she was simply "Ginny," but when in her chair behind the four-foot dais and flanked by the other four board members, she took her position quite seriously.

To her immediate right was Grady Laverd, a local farmer. On her left was Lucien Violette, the town's Farm Family Insurance agent who worked out of an office at the back of his garage. The other two members, Bill Conk and Lillian Meschovitzin, recently installed in last year's election, said little at meetings. Grady was known for his common sense, and Lucien was known for taking as many selfies as he could and posting them online as quickly as possible.

There were precious few details on the agenda. The first item read simply, "Personal issue," which Tom took to mean "Personnel issue."

"We begin with item number one," Ginny said.

Too quickly, Lucien said, "I move we move into executive session."

Bill reflexively said, "Second."

And the board was gone into a back room. When they returned thirty minutes later, they sat, and glanced at each other.

Lucien said, "I move we move back into regular session."

Bill said, "Second."

"We'll table that issue for now," Ginny said.

Nothing. No information. Tom rubbed his face. Newest reporter on staff, and these sorts of meetings were all his now.

"Next item," Ginny said. She looked at the young man seated to Tom's right, and said, "We're ready, Mr. Trottel."

The item listed on the agenda read only, "Beaver dam issue— Mr. Kyle Trottel, State of NH." It quickly became clear that some beavers had built a dam in an inconvenient place. Mr. Kyle Trottel, appearing to be in his early 20s, was an engineer sent from the state government in Concord. The road and dam had created a "V," holding back what the young engineer estimated was 10 acre-feet of water.

"What is an acre-foot?" Ginny asked.

"A good amount of water," Grady said.

"How much?" Lucien asked.

"So, an Olympic-sized pool might be a couple acre feet," Trottel said.

"And this pond is 10 acre-feet?" Ginny asked.

"Approximately," Trottel said.

Some glances around the board. "And what do you propose?" Lucien asked.

"First, we trap and relocate the beavers," Trottel said.

Grady sighed and rubbed his eyes. His button-down shirt was

neat, but the cuffs were rolled, and instead of the necktie that Lucien wore, Grady had a well-loved ball cap on his head. Across his brow was the word, "Kubota."

Trottel continued. "As for the dam, I believe we can remove it without damaging the road."

Lucien asked, "Remove it, how?"

"Explosives," Trottel said.

Grady sat straight up and dropped his hands. Tom didn't know why the farmer would object to explosives; surely the man had, in his long experience, even used some. Of course, Tom thought he knew of two drywall hangers who would love to bid on the job.

The other members had picked up on Grady's body language and were looking his way, when Grady relaxed and took up the questioning.

"Mr. Trottel, have you actually been up to the site?" Grady asked.

"I have," Trottel said.

"That beaver dam and that road, and the pond they hold back, are well above the lake," Grady said.

"That's right. The water will move into the lake, where it should have been going all along," Trottel said.

"And you plan to remove the dam and let that water go down to the lake," Grady said.

"Right," Trottel said. The kid actually looked pleased, as if he had finally managed to get the simple farmer to understand the plan.

"Mr. Trottel, what about the camps?" Grady asked.

"Camps?" Trottel asked.

"If you remove that dam with dynamite or whatever, 10 acre-feet of water will rush down that slope and will flush, what, maybe five camps into the lake like turds," Grady said.

The other board members and a few older folks sitting behind Tom and Trottel laughed. Grady did not. The poor kid never stood a chance. It was painfully obvious that the young engineer had only considered removing the dam and returning the water to the lake without any thought to what might be between the dam and the lake.

"Maybe we could channel it somehow?" Trottel asked.

"Maybe," Grady said. He rubbed his eyes again.

There was a heavy pause, and then Ginny said, "I suggest we table the issue until Mr. Trottel can return with a plan to channel the water."

Trottel only nodded.

Tom was smiling and jotting notes. The beaver dam issue had been a surprise treat. Not only was there a legitimate issue, but also a local farmer had scored a laugh at an outsider's expense. Grady Laverd hadn't done it to look smart, but he also couldn't resist shining a little light on the absence of common sense. This sort of thing made for great ink in a local paper. Grady was sure to get some smiles and backslapping at Agway in the coming weeks, and Dennis was sure to be happy with this bit of news for local refrigerators.

Trottel sat and began packing his papers and laptop for the drive back to Concord.

19

Ashley was surprisingly interesting. The phone call notwithstanding, Tom had expected a vapid, sort of kiss-ass kid. He thought she would be the sort of rock-star high school student who never had a failure to learn from, with an artificially inflated GPA, and who was in for a devastating wake-up at university. She wasn't that at all. She was smart, yes, but with a dry, sophisticated wit. She was sweet, but not cloying. Her laugh was rich and subtle, and not the nervous titter he had anticipated.

"This is Tom. He's a reporter from the newspaper and he's writing about Wish Night," Ashley said, introducing him to other members of the National Honor Society from Portage Regional High School. Every one of them wore identical polo shirts with a small embroidered "NHS" on the left breast. They were all squeaky clean, but they weren't Stepford students. They formed a rainbow of multiculturalism, with obvious hipsters mixed among neomaxizoomdweebies and jocks. They nodded and smiled their hellos.

From a couple rooms away, in the restaurant/function area of the Lumberman Hotel, Tom could hear a live band playing a cover of Bob Seger. He studied the students' faces. They exuded optimism and hope. It was contagious. Tom couldn't help but smile back.

"Nice to meet you," a girl closest to Tom said. She had dark eyes and a bright smile, and was barely more than five feet tall.

"Nice to meet you all," Tom said. "Ashley, can we sit somewhere and talk?"

"Sure, no problem," Ashley said.

They moved to a small area that looked like a souvenir shop within the hotel. There were t-shirts, pennants, and koozies each with "New Hampshire" lettered across them and the dark tapered silhouette of the state itself. The walls were all knotty pine. They chose a bench, the back of which was a length of sapling—cut, sanded, and coated in several layers of polyurethane. Tom placed his recorder on the bench between them.

"Tell me about Wish Night," Tom said.

More people came in, smiling locals dressed in suits and little black dresses. Tom wished he knew more people from Portage. He guessed that the men who had just come in were insurance agents, loan officers, or real estate agents. They looked affable and comfortable. Their wives had a look of prom-night happiness.

Ashley said, "Well, Wish Night is when people get together for a fundraiser for local people who are sick. It started years ago when Kenny Langlois—he was just a kid then—was diagnosed with leukemia. His family didn't have a lot of money, and just the drives down to Boston for treatment were draining the family's resources. So, the people of Portage got together for the first Wish Night. They raised enough money to help the Langlois family out, and even paid their mortgage for a couple months."

"When was that?" Tom asked.

Ashley looked up toward the ceiling, thinking, and then said, "This is the 11th Wish Night, so, yeah, do the math." She smiled.

Tom smiled again. "How many people attend?"

"We have ten NHS students here because we figure we want

about one student for every ten attendees. About a hundred people come. Local business owners, mostly," Ashley said.

"How does Wish Night raise money?" Tom asked.

Ashley said, "The attendees pay for the tables, and the name of their businesses are displayed on the tables. So that's the first step in fundraising. People also donate items for an auction, and the NHS kids run a lottery with tickets drawn for other donated prizes."

"What kind of prizes can people win with the lottery?" Tom asked.

"All kinds of stuff. You can win a day rental of kayaks, or a gift certificate to a restaurant, or even a yoga session," Ashley said.

"People just come forward with the items?" Tom asked.

"Oh yeah! Well, really, there's a lady here who runs around working really hard getting people to donate stuff, especially for the auction," Ashley said.

"And the auction is tonight?" Tom asked.

"Right after dinner," Ashley said. She smiled broadly.

"Is there anything else I should know?" Tom asked. He lifted the recorder.

Ashley thought for a moment. "You know, some of the people in the audience, they aren't all business people. Some of the adults in the audience, they were actually once sick kids who were helped by Wish Night and grew up to be healthy adults, and now they come back each year to show how grateful they are. One lady, very pretty, has Cystic Fibrosis, and she had a double-lung transplant and they helped her."

"Can you tell me who she is?" Tom asked.

Ashley smiled broadly. "I dare you to try and figure out which one she is. She looks great."

Tom smiled. This kid was something else.

"I have to go do my thing," Ashley said. She stood and extended her hand. "It was very nice talking to you."

Tom rose and shook her hand. "You, too, Ashley."

She rejoined the NHS crew, and then they dispersed in pairs in all directions. Tom decided to find his table, and maybe get a glass of wine. The newspaper had a table, and Dennis would be there, so Tom had requested a different table. He told Dennis he wanted to blend in a bit, and he asked if another table might be found for him. He was generously offered a seat with Conk Furniture.

He found it straight away, shook hands with the people closest to his seat, but didn't attempt the gymnastics it would have required to shake the hands of everyone. The only person he recognized was Bill Conk, the town selectman. The table had a white cloth and the chairs had white slipcovers pulled over them. The entire décor could be lifted off and bleached the next day.

Tom left and purchased a glass of pinot noir. The pretty young barmaid poured a full glass, and then leaned forward to say, "That'll be $11.50." Tom paid, dropping the change in the tip glass.

He returned to the table, and sat beside Bill Conk. The music was impossibly loud. The Conk Furniture table was mercifully three tables away from the stage and dance floor, but still, when Bill leaned in to ask Tom something, he missed it the first time.

"I said, how do you like Portage?" Bill asked.

"It's nice. The people are great," Tom said.

"Nice people around here," Bill agreed. Then he swept his hand, while nodding his head, pointing out that by their very presence the locals were proving they were good people. And they were. There was a sincerity and warmth in the room that Tom had not felt in some time. These people weren't just putting it on; they were legitimately here to help. Sure, they wanted to dress up, drink with their friends, enjoy a dinner, and take selfies to show others that they had been here, but at its heart, Wish Night was simply an act of group generosity and kindness. Tom at first fought to hold onto his skepticism, but could not. He found himself smiling with people he didn't know. Conversation continued to be challenging because of the volume at which the band played, but overall, it was like taking a bath and washing away snark and cynicism. It felt good.

When it was time to eat, there was a massive spread of roast beef, salmon, vegetables and salads, fresh bread, and more wine. The desserts were decadent. NHS students came around selling long stemmed roses. And then, there was the auction.

The band finally took a break, and into welcome silence stepped the owner of the Lumberman Hotel, a local raconteur named Andy Caswell, whom many admired, and about whom many had their own funny stories.

Andy stepped onto the dance floor in a sweater vest, tie, and top hat. He was a man in his late 60s, clean-shaven with grey hair. He picked up a cordless microphone, and began the auction.

"Folks, remember, none of you are here to find a bargain. The idea is to raise money, not to win an item with the least amount bid," Andy said.

Ashley appeared carrying an oil painting, perhaps a two-foot square, of an eagle perched on a branch. Tom thought the painting might be worth $200.

"Let's start the bidding at $150," Andy said.

Hands around the room shot up. Tom guessed that some of the people with their hands up had never bought a painting in their lives, outside of Wish Night.

Andy kept pointing at high-bidders and raising the price until he'd exhausted bids on this first item. "Alright, I've got $350 going once, twice, sold! There you go, Bobby, the painting's yours. And that's how this game is played folks, well done. Well done."

The next item was 18 yards of loam.

Someone called out, "Delivered?"

Andy laughed and said, "I tell you what. I'll deliver it myself. I'll throw that in."

Bids ran up into the hundreds of dollars quickly, and Andy added mid-bidding, "Well, I'll have it delivered, as long as you live in New Hampshire."

There was laughter. Tom was grinning. The open-handedness was infectious. Tom wished he could bid $500 on 18 yards of loam, but he didn't have $100 to spare, and he didn't think the other tenants at the Cooper Building would appreciate a pile of dirt, probably the size of eight parked cars, in the parking lot.

Tom went for another glass of wine. This time, instead of $11.50, it was $12.00. He laughed. He dropped the change in the tips, but then he realized that the barmaid was paying the difference. He pulled another couple dollars from his pocket and dropped it in the tips as well. He returned to his table as the auction ended. The band returned. He hadn't yet finished his wine when a woman from the next table asked him to dance. He glanced at her table, and easily identified her husband by the look of indulgence. The man was a portly, middle-aged man who clearly wasn't a huge fan of dancing. Tom nodded, and followed the woman to the crowded dance floor. Most of those dancing were women in their 30s and 40s, hands and dresses raised, grins, occasional whoops of joy. Pure fun. The woman dancing with Tom was in her mid-forties, a candy-apple-red form-fitting dress, and very pretty. Dark curls fell across her shoulders. She danced with Tom, not just in front of him, taking his hand, pulling him closer, pushing him away. All innocent, just fun with the music. More cheers, barely audible above the rendition of "Sweet Home Alabama," and now shoes were being kicked off the dance floor as many of the women chose to dance in bare feet instead. Tom danced. He danced, and felt free, and happy. He glanced around the floor, trying to guess which was the pretty woman who had had her ruined lungs surgically replaced. There was no way to know. It was all just music, and generosity, and joy. The very best of a small New England town.

20

Tom lay in bed with the manuscript "Tupac Was the Buddha" once more, flipped to his sticky-note bookmark, and read:

When the United States invaded Afghanistan, and then Iraq for a second time, the president was a Baby Boomer who had missed his own generation's war in Vietnam. The majority of the soldiers fighting on the ground were Millennials. Coming in the intervening years was Generation X's war.

I went to the desert, and participated in the first Gulf War. Near the end of the ground invasion, I was one of two intelligence sergeants chosen to go out to a captured bunker complex and see what we could find.

When I arrived, I stepped out of the Humvee and was approached by a filthy soldier, wearing boots, camouflage pants, and a flak vest over nothing else. No helmet, no t-shirt, no sunglasses. His dog tags swung from his neck. His body looked hard, but his dirt-caked face was round, and his hair was too long. I walked toward him, holding my rifle low, my helmet was on but the chinstrap was not snapped.

As we came together, he lit a cigarette. He did not offer me one. He pointed at our feet and said, "Don't step on those. They're mines."

Looking down between my feet, I saw three brown prongs protruding from the earth. I looked back toward the Humvee and saw that I'd walked past a dozen of them. "They'll blow your fuckin' foot off," he said, took another drag, turned around and walked away. As he went, I scanned the area carefully. The little protrusions of the mines were everywhere, like dandelions in a park. I walked carefully between them until I came to one of the doors to the underground complex, and proceeded down the stairs. There were fresh vegetables, fresh tomatoes in particular, on a table below an enormous painting of Saddam Hussein. We hadn't had a bit of fresh vegetables in months.

I spent the day collecting this piece of electronics and discarding that piece, and then I made my way back to the surface. The sun was setting by this time. The sky was orange; the sand was tinted that way. All around me were mounds disguising the entrances to the massive complex beneath my feet. Not a soul was in sight; the others were all below ground.

I couldn't see plumes of smoke from the well fires, but even the setting sun appeared greasy. Then, emerging from behind a mound to my right was a mare and her foal. They were both dreadfully skinny, with every rib apparent. I stood there, smoking a cigarette, and watched as they entered the minefield, and strolled through it. Every step the mare took seemed to require a conscious effort. The foal stayed behind her, just to one side. Each time a hoof came to rest on the ground, I expected a mine to blow that hoof off. I took another drag and watched as she silently and slowly led her damned offspring through that minefield.

They passed through the entire miniature forest of prongs

without setting off a single mine, and then disappeared behind a mound on the far side. I flicked my cigarette butt in the direction they had gone. There was no food out that way. There was no water. There was no hope out there.

I rubbed my face, pulled the canteen from the small of my back, took a sip and let some run down my chin and throat, soaking my collar. I missed New Hampshire. In that godforsaken place, I longed for a sunset on Squam Lake, or the sound of ducks, the taste of real maple syrup, and even the smell of skunks.

I stood in a spot where, if not for the mounds of earth, I could see 15 miles in every direction, and yet the air tasted stale and the sky was a weight I could not shrug off.

The war had lasted mere weeks. We had come a half-a-million strong, with the best training and equipment, with an army designed to confront the Soviets. We had unleashed it on an army said to be the world's fourth largest, but it had been so uneven that many of Generation X's warriors had been perversely disappointed. We had come in with tanks and helicopters and in 100 hours, we had destroyed the Iraqi army in a way that armies had not been stamped out since perhaps the Third Punic War, except on a larger scale and at 50 miles per hour. It had not been a push-button war. It had been dirty and fierce, with spirited opposition coming from the Republican Guard divisions. Still, it had been over quickly and decisively. So quickly, it caught us all by surprise.

Near the waters of the Persian Gulf, miles of oil wells burned. Out in the desert, captured chemical weapons were being recklessly destroyed. Back home, veterans of the war in Vietnam were already rallying to ensure our homecoming would be friendlier than theirs had been, when the Baby

Boomers had turned on their own. We would feel both gratitude and guilt about being welcomed home so warmly. I stood there. Various pieces of Iraqi electronic junk in the rucksack at my feet. I stood there, looking out at the darkening minefield, and lit another cigarette. Surreal. A puppy barked somewhere, one of several we had found. The Iraqis, worried about nerve gas, had used them just as canaries had once been used in coal mines.

My eyes stung. The days-old laceration in my right forearm, itchy with healing, hastily stitched, was filthy and sore. I exhaled the smoke through my nose.

I knew I would be out of sync after all this. That I, and the others who had seen man's madder face, would be slightly out of sync with the rest of Generation X afterwards. While they had aged a week in dorm rooms and apartments with cheap beer and CNN, those of us who had actually been in the fight had aged more quickly. We had shaken off the last of our innocence. We knew even then we'd never quite fit in again, but we resolved to hide it and fake it, and we prayed that the rest of Generation X would play along.

Tom closed the manuscript. In 1991, during Desert Storm, Tom had been a junior in high school. He remembered images of the Iraqi tracer rounds streaking into the black sky over Baghdad, fired in blind hope of slowing the airstrikes. He remembered the oil fires, ink-black smoke roiling into the desert sky, lakes of liquid oil on the sand. He remembered bombsite video of smart munitions being guided in through windows or striking bridges. He remembered being in awe of the machinery of war. He thought of the soldiers as a like-minded mass, working in unison, like ants or a swarm of wasps, and then marching in parades like smiling lemmings. He hadn't considered the individual soldier's experience, nor had he wondered if there might be a less-than-obvious reaction to being welcomed home with open arms and celebration.

Tom wondered what the author would advise him to do. Would he tell Tom to suck up his whining and do the best he could? He was being paid to do a job, and neither the tasks nor the conditions were anything like those described in the manuscript. Or would he advise him to shake off the yoke and be free? Perhaps to question every purpose and every action? Tom was a member of Generation X, just as the author was, but Tom still was not sure of his place within it.

21

The next evening, Tom heard laughter. He stared at the wall between his and Ben's apartment. He heard it again. Two men, struggling to keep quiet, were laughing. Tom had just left the couch to go to bed, but there was something inviting—and perhaps a bit intriguing—about the laughter. After Wish Night, he was jonesing for more of the warmth of human kindness.

He walked out onto the balcony and stepped to Ben's door. Ben was speaking now, and the other man laughing. Tom knocked, and then entered. Ben was sitting on the floor next to Miguel, their backs against the sofa. Both men were, as they looked up, at once startled and confused. Then, with recognition flashing across their faces, they collapsed together in a fit of resumed laughter. The room was thick with pot smoke. A glass bong sat on the coffee table in front of them; the bowl and bong were a translucent dark blue, while the stem and mouthpiece were clear. A bottle of absinthe was also on the table with two glasses each containing a remaining swallow of the green liquid.

"Close the door, man!" Ben said, and Miguel rubbed his eyes. Tom closed the door.

"Well, c'mon, sit down," Ben said. He motioned to the floor on the other side of the coffee table. Tom knelt there.

"Want a hit?" Miguel said, dropping his hands from his eyes.

Ben stood. "Hook him up. I'll get another glass."

"You're out of sugar cubes," Miguel said.

"We'll fuckin' rough it," Ben said, and both men dissolved into laughter again. Ben stopped walking to hold himself up, hands on knees. Tom felt left far behind, and he desperately wanted to catch up. He hadn't smoked weed since he had split a single joint four ways in his last year of college. He was willing to try to make up for lost time. Miguel packed the bowl, got up on his knees, and turned the bong so that the mouthpiece was in Tom's face. Ben returned with another glass and poured three full glasses of absinthe. The drink he pushed toward Tom was clear and bright green, while the other two were slightly milky. Miguel slid the bowl into place on the bong's stem. He waited for Tom to place his mouth on the bong. Tom did and watched as Miguel applied flame to the bowl.

"Pull, man, pull," Miguel said.

Ben snickered, and said, "Suck on it, man."

Tom inhaled and watched the lower chamber fill with smoke. Miguel lifted the bowl from the bong, released the smoke, and the white rushed up the tube into Tom's lungs. Cool and smooth. He held the smoke, as he remembered to do, and then let it go.

"Right on, man," Miguel said. He adjusted the contents of the bowl with the non-working end of the lighter, slid the bowl back into the bong, and lit it. Tom took another lung-full.

Through the smoke he was exhaling, Tom saw Ben raise his glass of absinthe. Miguel followed suit. Tom reached for his glass, carefully, his judgment of distance already slightly impaired.

"To the reporter," Ben said.

"Capturing the truth," Miguel said.

"Whoever he may be," Tom said.

They all laughed at this. Tom sipped; the licorice flavor was powerful and pleasant.

"Okay, Tom, so what are you doing here?" Ben said.

"Apparently, getting fucked up," Tom said. "I heard you guys laughing and thought I'd come see what was up."

"Oh sorry, man, were we too loud?" Miguel said half-voiced, half-whisper.

"It's all good," Tom said, "And getting better." He could feel the effects in the skin of his face, his eyelids. He took another sip of the absinthe, a longer one.

"I didn't know you smoked," Miguel said.

"I don't," Tom said. "Is this what you guys do? Sit here, looking at each other, getting high?"

"We aren't just staring at each other, man, we're talking about shit," Ben said.

"Like what?"

"What were we talking about?" Miguel asked.

Both Ben and Miguel considered this for a long minute and then collapsed into another laughter-hug.

"Hey, can I get that fucked up, too, please?" Tom asked.

Miguel helped him through another bowl of pot.

"There's freedom in it, isn't there?" Miguel asked.

"Totally," Tom said.

"That's it. We were talking about freedom, man," Ben said.

"Right," Miguel said.

"What kind of freedom? Like, your rights?" Tom asked.

"Yeah, man, exactly. Like freedom *from* the press," Miguel said, with heavy emphasis on 'from' rather than 'of.' He laughed.

"Yeah, freedom *from* religion," Ben said, and they both laughed.

"Freedom *from* speech," Tom said, and both of the others stopped laughing.

"Man, you don't need freedom from speech. You need to be able to express yourself," Miguel said.

"You mean like freedom from having to say something?" Ben asked.

"Free from trying to sound like I know what the fuck I'm talking about. Free from people looking to me for answers," Tom said.

"Answers are good, though," Miguel said.

"I haven't got them," Tom said.

"Opinions, man, opinions are disastrous," Ben said.

"Voltaire said that," Tom said.

Miguel said, "Cool, man. Lay some Voltaire on me."

"He said that opinions were worse than plague and earthquakes," Tom said.

"Opinion has caused more trouble on this little planet than plagues or earthquakes," Ben said, eyes closed.

Tom lifted his glass, and said, "Keep your opinions to yourself."

"Yeah, shut the fuck up," Miguel said.

"No opining," Ben said.

Tom finished the glass. The lights were beginning to morph into a starburst effect.

"So, when will you interview us?" Miguel asked.

"I'm doing it right now," Tom said.

Miguel set up the bong for himself. His eyes were moving from Ben to Tom and back again. Ben pushed a bowl of chips across the table. Tom reached out and grabbed a handful, and Ben refilled the glasses.

"What made you want to write about us?" Ben asked. Miguel held the smoke for an impossibly long time before adding to the cloud in the room.

"I didn't. My boss assigned these stories. To get a look at

Portage from the points of view of a bunch of locals," Tom said.

"But you're not hating it," Ben said. "You're even expanding the project." He took a sip without a toast this time. Tom reached for his glass, too, the light spectacular along the glass's edge now. He drank a bit more than a sip.

"It grew on me, you know?" Tom said. "Like, I switched sides. I thought you people were all nuts, but now it feels like being in that office is crazy, like it's trapping me. I don't know if I'm going to write that longer piece on Brynn, though."

Ben said, "Why not?"

Tom said, "What's the point?"

"You mean, like, what if you write it, and it gets printed, but no one reads it? Like, they skip it?" Ben asked. "Then you will have stayed trapped working for the man for nothing for all this extra time."

"At least you'll have written it, though," Miguel said.

"You don't need the newspaper for that," Ben said.

Tom was confused now. The weed wasn't helping. Was it important that Brynn's story get written if not printed? Probably not. Fuck it. The hell with all of it.

"Have you even interviewed Brynn yet?" Miguel asked.

"Not really," Tom said.

"She might not have cooperated," Miguel said.

"She wants her story told, before it's too late," Ben said.

Miguel's face seemed to harden a bit. "Grim, man. Grim."

"Did Mike say anything about Brynn?" Ben asked.

"I just learned about them," Tom said. "Has that been going on for a while?"

"Not very long," Miguel said. "Mike says they're just fuck-buddies. Like, maybe he's just using her. Kind of fucked up, really, because she's messed up, you know?"

Tom remembered Brynn saying she wished men saw her as more than that. He felt a new pang of sympathy for her.

Ben seemed to sense this. "You're completely harshing the buzz."

"Sorry, man," Miguel said. "You know, you can free yourself anytime you want to, man."

"More Voltaire," Ben said.

"Ah please, man, everybody says that," Miguel said, and all three of them laughed.

"Are you guys going to the cookout?" Tom asked.

Both laughed.

"What else're we going to do?" Miguel asked.

Tom asked, "Why do you guys hold it so late in the year? It's late autumn. It's not going to be warm out."

Ben said, "People travel in the summer. Have to wait until everyone is here."

"Think Hitch will go this year?" Tom asked.

Ben pulled hard on the bong, released and inhaled the smoke, and then exhaled his answer. "No fucking way. Hitch never goes to any of those things."

"What's up with that guy, anyway?" Tom asked. "No one seems to know anything about him."

"He just comes and goes, you know what I mean?" Miguel said.

Tom nodded, but then said, "I don't get it."

"What?" Ben said.

"The guy isn't a shut-in. We see him all the time," Tom said.

"So?" Miguel asked.

"So, in all the years you all have lived together in this building, no one has stopped him to have a conversation?" Tom asked.

"What the hell would we say?" Ben asked.

"I don't know," Tom said. "How about, 'Hey, Mr. Hitch, what's with the wetsuit?'"

"No way, man," Miguel said.

"Why not?" Tom asked.

Miguel and Ben paused, looked at each other, and then Miguel said, "Because, man, he might answer."

"I don't get it," Tom said.

Ben said, "Look, man, right now Mr. Hitch is the freaky mystery dude in a wetsuit one day, and then he's on rollerblades the next. If we ask him about it, he might have a rational answer, but we don't want him to be rational. We don't want to find out he is a product tester from Kravnik's Sporting Goods or something. Like, he won't be a mystery anymore."

Miguel said, "Yeah, like who wants to solve all the mysteries?"

Tom motioned for the bong. Miguel packed, lit, and lifted once more. Everything was just making so much more sense now, and the lights were really amazing.

"So, you and Winnie are a thing now?" Miguel asked.

Tom said, "She's pretty cool."

"A good one," Ben said, nodding.

"Will you be a couple at the cookout? Because Brynn might take that hard," Miguel said.

"I haven't led her on," Tom said. "Besides, she has Mike."

"Brynn doesn't want you, man," Ben said. "She just wants 'the romance thing.' She sees you as the nice guy she can't seem to get."

"I don't know what to do about that," Tom said.

"Nothing you can do," Miguel said. "Just keep love in your heart, man, and be kind. All you can do."

"Do you have a girlfriend?" Tom asked.

Miguel pointed at his own head. "No room in here; it's busy enough."

"Can you hear voices now?" Tom asked. "Does smoking pot clear the voices out of your head?"

"No way! Makes them worse, if anything," Miguel said, patting the bong. "But this helps me with my anxiety. I think, anyway"

"You?" Tom asked Ben.

Ben shifted a bit. "I've been seeing someone, but it's complicated."

"Kids?" Tom asked.

"She's married," Miguel said.

Ben shot a look at Miguel, and the latter clammed up. Ben then asked, "So what are you going to do about work?"

"You know what?" Tom said. "Fuck them. I'm never going back. I'll just write the stories I want to write."

"How will you pay the bills?" Miguel asked.

"Is McDonald's hiring?" Tom asked.

Ben said, "Find your own thing, man. I've got the McNuggets covered."

Miguel giggled.

Tom, still sitting on the floor, leaned back a bit and his elbow gave way. He fell halfway to the floor before catching himself. Miguel and Ben burst into another round of laughter. Tom laughed, too. He was trying so hard to keep his eyes open while laughing that his eyebrows felt like they had lifted halfway to his hairline, as if his eyebrows were attempting to tow his eyelids open.

"I'm fucked up," Tom announced.

"No shit," Miguel said, still giggling.

Ben poured more absinthe and handed a glass to Tom.

Tom asked, "Think I should have more?"

"No fucking way," Ben said. "But go ahead and drink it."

Tom did. The lights weren't only starbursts now, but were actually streaking when he turned his head.

"Cool," Tom whispered.

Miguel nodded. Ben whispered back. "Cool."

22

He couldn't eat lunch. He hadn't had breakfast. He had no appetite. He had seemingly irreversible dry-mouth, and a pounding headache. Damn absinthe. His dreams had blurred right into his first waking minutes before fading, and he had stumbled around ever since. He opened the fridge and saw the sausages he had picked up for the cookout. He winced. At that moment, anything more than a Tums sandwich seemed ambitious. He grabbed a bottle of water. It was actually too cold, and it made his headache worse.

He brushed his teeth for the second time that day. He hopped into the shower. That helped. A pair of comfy jeans and a hoodie. He sat at the laptop and checked his email. There was one email from Dennis. It had no greeting and no sign-off, just a single sentence that read, "Should we expect you today?"

Tom deleted the email and read the unfinished piece on Mike and Matt. There really was no story there, not the one he could write anyway. Why bother? Why force it? He had been right last night. He wasn't going to write any more of this shit. He was all set with going in to work anymore.

Tom heard laughter down below. He held his head. He had followed the sound of laughter the night before, and now he regretted it. He closed the laptop, returned to the fridge, grabbed the package of thick sausages, and headed for the parking lot. He'd bring the sausages, the guys could cook them up, and whoever wanted them could have them. Once on the balcony, he could see the building's residents milling about. He caught bits of the Brynn's and Winnie's conversation below.

"There he is," Winnie said.

"Looks like he had a rough night," Brynn said.

Winnie laughed. "He's a pretty good guy. I think he's just evolving."

Brynn asked, "Like a butterfly to a caterpillar?"

Winnie said, "He's just finding out who he became, while he wasn't paying attention and in spite of himself, and he's beginning to consider who he might be instead."

Tom rubbed his face as he walked. *'Who he became?' What was that supposed to mean?*

Brynn said, "I'm just teasing. He was very sweet that night I fell."

Fell. She always says it that way. Tom made his way down the stairs and handed the meat to Rich at the grill.

Tom said, "Here, a donation. I'm not hungry."

"Amateur."

Tom turned to find Ben grinning at him.

"I'm dying," Tom said.

"I think you'll make it," Ben said.

Just then Miguel came flying around the corner on his unicycle, his face covered in a huge grin, a cigarette clenched in his teeth, and his thin hair streaming behind.

Brynn was still talking to Winnie. So far, so good. Both women lifted polite little waves to Tom. He only smiled back, and even the smile hurt. Marie joined the girls then. Becky stood off a bit by herself, sipping on a glass of wine. Everyone else had red Solo cups, but Becky had an enormous glass with a thin stem and base. This she set on the hood of the Lennox brothers' pickup, but had to hold onto it for fear it would tip over. The Lennox brothers themselves sat on the lowered tailgate of their truck, talking to each other, leaning up against the tarp-covered contents of the bed. Ben walked over to them, and Tom followed.

"I've got some hot dogs ready here," Rich announced.

No one responded, nor showed any interest.

"You guys working today?" Ben asked.

"No, but we're leaving in about fifteen minutes," Mike said.

"You'll miss the cookout," Tom said.

"You working today?" Matt asked.

Tom wasn't sure to whom Matt was speaking.

"Day off today," Ben said.

"Me, too," Tom said.

Matt and Mike laughed. "When isn't it a day off for you?"

"I was at the office just yesterday," Tom said.

Mike said, "Yeah, I heard you working at Winnie's when I walked by." The brothers laughed.

Tom glanced over at Winnie and Brynn, and then turned back to Mike. "Believe me, I could hear you through the door at Brynn's," Tom said. "Not to mention, through my ceiling."

Mike stopped laughing, but Matt only laughed harder. As for Ben, he wasn't laughing. He was exchanging stares with Becky Kapel. Becky guzzled the rest of her wine. She went over to the folding table and filled the glass once more from a large box labeled, "Franzia."

Miguel passed behind her on his unicycle, this time cigarette in hand. He was singing, "Nobody's Fault but Mine," doing his best Robert Plant.

"He can really move on that thing," Tom said. Ben didn't

respond, he was still staring at Becky. The Lennox brothers noticed as well.

"Hey, man, snap out of it," Matt said.

Ben slowly turned away from Becky. Tom saw her raise her glass to Ben's back, and then drain the glass as a child might drink fruit punch. What the fuck?

Marie passed between Ben and Becky as she approached them.

"Here comes E.T.," Matt said.

"Tom, I want to thank you," Marie said.

"For the story?" Tom asked.

"The local morning show asked me on as a guest. They want me to come on the radio as one of those experts," Marie said.

"Which show?" Matt asked.

"Glenn and the Morning Crew," she said, beaming.

Not good. They would surely hold her up for public ridicule. But hadn't he done the same?

"Are you sure you want to go on?" Mike asked. "Some people might think you have a screw loose."

"Yeah, it's not like that's a science show or something," Matt said.

"They promised me today, a nice lady from the station named Lisa, she promised me today that those boys would be polite," Marie said.

Then Becky came over. It was immediately clear that her drinking had not been limited to the two Tom had seen her finish. She laid her palm flat on Ben's chest.

"I need to talk to you," Becky said, her face clearly too close to Ben's.

Ben immediately glanced at Rich's back, who had no idea where his wife was.

"Not right now," Ben said.

"I need to talk to you," Becky said.

"You're drunk," Ben said. "Maybe we should talk later."

Rich said loudly, "I still have hot dogs, they're turning black, come and get 'em."

"Stop brushing me off. I need to talk to you, away from all these people," Becky pleaded.

"Becky, stop. This isn't cool. Let's talk later," Ben said.

Becky stepped back and stared at Ben's knees. "Goddammit! You fuck me and fuck me, and now I need you and you won't even talk to me?" She threw her glass at his feet. It exploded into a million shards and a splash of pink wine.

Rich spun on his heels, spatula in one hand, long-handled fork in the other. The Lennox brothers sprang off the tailgate. Ben dropped his chin to his chest. Miguel came zooming by, but this time, not smiling.

Oh no.

"What the hell did you just say?" Rich asked.

"Fuck you, too, Richard. Except you can't, can you?" Becky said. She tried to storm away, but her short legs became crossed and she fell, seated, on the asphalt in just about the same spot where Brynn had landed when she had leapt from the balcony.

Tom felt as though everything were moving much faster than he could track. Rich charged at Ben, just as the Lennox brothers rushed in to intercept him. Ben never moved. Brynn and Winnie ran to Becky to help her up. Marie stared at the sky. There was a clamor of shouting and cursing. The collision between Rich and the Lennoxes was impressive. The sixty-seven-year-old very nearly came over the top of the two robust young men, who wrapped him in their arms, and then shouted at Ben.

"Get out of here, man!" Matt said.

Rich was shouting again and again. "I'm going to fucking kill you! I swear to Christ! I'll tear your fucking head off!"

"Go! Go!" Mike said.

Ben did not move. He had not even lifted his chin from his chest. Winnie and Brynn no sooner had Becky on her feet than she pushed toward Rich. "Stop it! Stop it!"

Ben looked up, his face flushed red, and something seemed to snap. Ben sprinted toward the backs of the brothers.

"You sanctimonious idiot! You don't even deserve a woman like that!" Ben said.

Matt released Rich and turned to catch the onrushing Ben. Each brother now had one of the potential combatants.

"Don't you hurt him, you big gorilla!" Becky shrieked. It was all Brynn and Winnie could do to hold onto Becky. Tom finally seemed to regain control of his body and stepped forward to help Matt with Ben.

"She's a creature of passion, with a loving heart!" Ben said. "You don't deserve her, you cold-hearted, selfish *cabron!*"

Rich made a renewed effort to reach Ben, and Mike had to lift and hold the man in the air in a bear hug to stop him.

Tom was shouting, "Ben! Enough! Enough!"

The entire scene was utter chaos. Just then, Tom saw Miguel swing around and approach at great speed. He made the unicycle hop once, and then with a bounce, he landed on his feet in the bed of the Lennox brothers' pickup. He was holding the unicycle in his right hand, and his cigarette in his left.

"Hey! Everyone! Stop! Let's just stop! Love can fix this! Violence isn't the way! Let's just stop!" Miguel shouted.

Marie was now calling to the aliens, palms upward, eyes closed. "Just come back to us now. We need you to save us."

"Hey! Stop!" Miguel shouted. "This is no way to be!" Mike and Matt had not seen Miguel until he tossed the unicycle to the asphalt, and then he dropped the cigarette at his foot. When Matt saw this, he released Ben and ran toward Miguel and the truck.

"Miguel! Get out of there!" Matt said as he ran.

Tom, left to manage Ben by himself, was being pushed backward when the bed of the truck exploded. Everyone in the parking lot was thrown to the ground. Matt, who had been rushing to save Miguel, was almost to the truck when the explosives in the bed went off. Matt flew back as if tossed by his head. There was no real fireball to speak of, more just a flash and shockwave. The windows in the truck blew around the lot, and the apartment windows blew into the building. Miguel was thrown upward and collided with the second floor balcony. Tom didn't see him fall.

The ringing in Tom's ears was all he could hear. As he sat up, he saw Mike rushing to his brother's side. Ben was lying beside Tom, rolling from side to side, but with no obvious blood or injury. Tom got to his feet and rushed over to Winnie and Brynn. Both had nicks and cuts from the windows of the pickup truck. Becky was on her back, with Rich standing at her side. The first voice Tom could make out was hers.

"I'm so sorry. I'm so sorry," Becky said. She appeared more repentant than injured, and when Rich seemed to realize this, he stepped away from her, leaving her to cry.

Marie was walking around in a circle, apparently bewildered and stunned.

With each passing second, Tom could hear more and more, including sirens in the distance. His head hurt, and his shoulder ached. He got moving. He passed the brothers. Matt was writhing in pain.

"You're going to be okay," Mike said to Matt.

"I can't see! I'm blind! I'm blind!" Matt said.

Tom moved past the burning truck and arrived at Miguel's

body. He dropped to his knees to try to help. First aid, remember first aid.

"There's nothing you can do."

Tom looked up. It was Mr. Hitch. He was standing in a drug-rug poncho with a sombrero hanging on his back. Tom looked back down. Hitch was right. Miguel's eyes were open, but blood red. His neck was clearly broken. Much of his clothing was missing. His exposed skin was burned black. His left hand and both feet were missing. Hitch walked away, but did not go upstairs. He sat on a section of concrete wall and stared at his feet.

Tom surveyed the scene. Ben was on all fours. The Kapels were apart, and Becky was still quietly weeping. Marie, Brynn, and Winnie were in a huddle. The brothers were hugging. Hitch sat silently. Miguel's body lay where it had fallen.

What the hell was he doing here? Why was he with these people? The smoke from the truck rolled upward and obscured the door to his apartment. He looked at Miguel once more.

What was he doing in this parking lot? Where was he supposed to be? Was he supposed to be here?

An ambulance arrived, soon followed by a police cruiser, and then fire trucks. The red and blue lights splashed across the walls and into the smoke. People were now massing to gawk from the sidewalk. The police tried to chase them off, for fear of another explosion, but they only backed away a bit.

"You were all very lucky," a police officer said. The cop appeared so young, Tom was sure he owned shoes older than the boy.

"All?" Tom asked. Miguel's body was covered in a grey, wool blanket inside a yellow-police tape perimeter.

Tom relayed his version of events, withholding that he had had knowledge, gained during his interview, of the Lennox's hobby.

"You've taken the photos, why not take the body out of here now?" Tom asked.

"Waiting for the ATF," the cop said. "Waiting to hear if they want to get involved. Their turf."

"The ATF," Tom repeated. Federal authorities. A bomb. It occurred to Tom that the Lennox brothers won't be looked at as a couple redneck brothers with a dangerous hobby that accidentally killed a neighbor. They will be charged with constructing, possessing, and transporting explosive devices. State and federal laws had been broken.

The brothers apparently realized the stakes just as Tom did.

"It was all mine," Matt said, blindfolded with a bandage. Despite the IV and whatever meds he had been given, he was clearly still in a lot of pain.

"He didn't know anything about it," Mike said.

Tom wondered again what he was doing here with these people.

Winnie slowly approached. "You okay?"

Tom nodded. He scanned for Brynn. She was wrapped in a blanket, sitting under a light as the last of the sunlight faded.

"Did I shift the balance here?" Tom suddenly asked.

"What?"

"You all lived here, and Brynn was attempting suicide on a regular basis, but even then, no one actually died," Tom said.

"You think you're to blame for this?" Winnie asked.

Matt was taken away in an ambulance. Mike was handcuffed and placed in a cruiser. Brynn followed him to the car, crying, and kissing him before he was stuffed into it. As the cruiser pulled away, Brynn ran upstairs, still wrapped in the blanket, and disappeared into her apartment.

Tom said nothing. He turned and walked to the road. Winnie

did not follow him. As he got to the sidewalk, Allan met him there.

"What the hell happened?" Allan asked. He immediately began taking photos.

Tom walked past him. He left Allan behind, walked down the hill, walked through the grassy common, and made his way to the office. A few people were still there, including Dennis, who was on the phone at Allan's desk. Tom still said nothing and walked to his own desk. He sat.

"Were you at the explosion?" Dennis asked.

"What am I doing here?" Tom asked.

Dennis looked worried that Tom had suffered a head injury. In a way, he had. Dennis hung up the phone.

"Are you alright? Do you need an ambulance?" Dennis asked.

"I just left one," Tom said.

"What happened?"

Tom said, "The explosives in the back of a pickup truck went up when Miguel dropped his unicycle and his cigarette." His voice was flat.

"Why were there explosives in the back of a truck?" Dennis asked.

"They liked to blow up furniture. And old cars," Tom said.

"Who?" Dennis asked.

"The Lennox brothers," Tom said.

"They had explosives? Why?" Dennis asked. "Don't they hang sheetrock? Why would they need explosives?"

"Balance," Tom said.

Dennis said, "We should get you to the hospital."

"I'm fine," Tom said. "Oh, but all that is off the record."

"What is?" Dennis asked.

"That stuff about the Lennox brothers. They told me not to tell anyone," Tom said.

Another police car rushed by outside the newspaper, heading for the apartments, siren blaring. It seemed these cops were late to the scene, but didn't want to miss the chance to use the siren. Those opportunities didn't present themselves often in Portage.

"Was anyone hurt?" Dennis asked. "I mean, I assume Miguel was."

"Miguel's dead. Matt or Mike can't see, I can't remember which," Tom said.

Allan came into the office. Dennis pointed to Tom, and Allan nodded.

"Did you get anything?" Dennis asked.

"A couple photos. And a quote from a cop. Someone's dead. I'll call for the rest," Allan said. "Is he alright?"

Tom said, "I'm alright."

Dennis licked his lips and rocked forward in the seat. "Tom, do you think you could write the story? Of the explosion?"

Tom blinked.

"Dennis, the guy is a victim," Allan said. "Could we hold off just a bit?"

"But we'll have an angle the dailies won't have," Dennis said. "Besides, Tom, your story will probably get picked up. A lot of people will see it."

"Leave him alone," Allan said.

"Tom, it would be a way for people to find out about Miguel. For people to know what kind of person he was," Dennis said.

So transparent. So disgusting. Tom could feel his rage building.

"Don't let him be just a victim of a freak incident. He'll be forgotten in a week. Write the story. You can also tell people about the brothers. You might even be able to help them. I've seen newspaper stories change the outcomes of trials. You're the only one who could do it," Dennis said.

Tom only stared at him. Dennis licked his lips again. Like some sort of rodent. Some sort of nervous, trembling, rodent— salivating at the misfortune of others.

"You can have the entire front page," Dennis said.

"Enough!" Allan said.

Dennis glanced at Allan and then added, "And the center truck, if you want it."

Tom felt the anger, suppressed until that moment, seemingly explode from his chest and drag him forward over his own desk and onto Allan's. Dennis pushed himself backward, his face twisted in terror. Allan grabbed Tom by the back of his shirt, and when Tom fell forward onto the top of Allan's desk, Allan fell on top of him.

"Stop! Stop!" Allan shouted.

Tom stopped struggling. He could feel the cool of the blotter against his cheek. He could smell the fake wooden desktop. The glow of the monitor fell across his face. He regained control of himself.

"Let me up," Tom said.

Allan stepped back, but Tom could feel the fist still wrapped in the back of his shirt. Tom stood. He looked at Dennis, with his chair rolled back to the wall.

"Fuck you and this job," Tom said.

He turned to leave. Dennis said nothing. Allan turned with him, and then Tom felt Allan's hand releasing his shirt. Tom stepped through the door and out onto the sidewalk with Allan close behind.

Tom stopped. "What do you want, Allan?"

Allan said, "What's next?"

Tom didn't know. "I'm going to see if I can get into my apartment."

"I mean, what's next?" Allan asked.

Tom faced him. "None of this matters anyway, right?"

Allan said nothing.

"I'm done, Allan. I don't know what's next. I'm not even sure what's been lost, but I know what's ended," Tom said. He turned and headed back up the hill toward the apartment. Maybe Winnie would know what to do next.

23

Local cops stood like spectators while state police and ATF agents walked throughout the area that had been the cookout. Miguel's body was gone. Cameras whirred. The building super was already boarding up Marie's windows. Tom caught a glimpse of her inside. She looked to be vacuuming. It was cool outside; the apartments wouldn't be warm.

Tom reached Winnie's door. There were no windowpanes, and he could hear people inside. Tom knocked and entered. Becky and Winnie were on the couch. Both had obviously been crying.

Tom moved to a chair, checked it for broken glass and, seeing none, fell into it. Becky sniffled. There were no pieces of glass on the floor either. Winnie must have cleaned up even more quickly than Marie had.

They all sat silently for long minutes before Tom asked, "Where is Rich?"

Becky's face twisted and she leaned into Winnie, crying into her shoulder. Winnie glared at Tom. He decided asking about Ben was probably equally bad. They all sat silently again.

"Marie was here for a little bit," Winnie offered. A safe person to talk about.

"Mr. Hitch went back inside his place, I suppose," Tom said. No one answered. Becky cried softly.

"What will happen to Mike and Matt?" Winnie asked.

Tom shifted in his seat. "They'll be charged, probably with both state and federal crimes."

Becky was still crying, but Tom could tell she had listened to his answer.

Tom asked, "Any news on Matt?"

Winnie said, "He'll make it, but they think he might be permanently blind. I got a text from Lonnie Jenks, the EMT."

Tom asked, "Does anyone know about Miguel's family? Someone to notify?"

"Cops said they'd take care of it," Winnie said.

"Still, it might be nice if someone could call," Tom said.

Becky turned. Her eyes were swollen and red, her face wet with tears. "Ben said he'd call Miguel's mother."

"So sad," Winnie said.

"Why did they have explosives in the back of their truck?" Becky asked. She knew about their hobby. She wasn't looking for a literal answer. "Poor Miguel. And now I've lost him."

Tom said, "Well, maybe you two could go to marriage counseling."

Winnie winced and Becky glared at Tom. Becky said, "Not Rich! I've lost *Ben*. He left me there, in the lot, and went to his apartment. His door is locked and curtains drawn. He won't answer his phone."

"Yeah, but Becky, I mean… you're like thirty years older than Ben," Tom said.

"Tom, shut up!" Winnie said. "Don't judge!"

"What do you know, huh?" Becky asked. "You can't pick who you fall in love with. It just happens."

Tom didn't say anything. Winnie said, "You're right, Becky. It'll be okay."

Becky said, "And you. *Mr. Reporter.* You come out of nowhere and you show up here and now look at all this mess."

Tom looked to Winnie's face, trying to read if she had told Becky about his earlier comments about throwing the karmic balance off. Winnie shook her head, apparently reading his mind and answering his question.

"You and Ben only began having an affair after I arrived?" Tom said.

Becky's face twisted up again, and she once again buried it in Winnie's shoulder.

"Asshole," Winnie hissed.

Well, if he was already an asshole… "Why didn't you just leave Rich and move in with Ben, if you two are so in love and all?"

Becky spun. "Because! A wife doesn't just leave her husband! Scripture says that we have to listen and obey. So I obeyed!"

Tom was about to point out the problem with adultery, vis-à-vis scripture, but Winnie held up one extended finger in warning, and Tom held his tongue.

Becky fell back into Winnie's chest.

Tom said, "I'm sorry, Becky."

Becky said, "But I know now I was wrong. I should have left Rich. It's been wrong for a long time. But now I've lost Ben, too." Winnie rocked her slowly. There was a quick knock and the door opened. It was the super.

"Everyone okay in here? I'm gonna board up these windows here, OK?" he asked.

Winnie nodded and the door closed. A piece of plywood was soon screwed into place behind Tom, leaving the room a bit darker, but the heating system immediately began to catch up, and the temperature quickly rose in the apartment.

"Are all the windows broken?" Tom asked.

"First and second floor," Winnie said.

Tom nodded. He would have broken glass to pick up in his apartment as well.

"Miguel was such a nice guy," Winnie said.

Tom remembered being in Ben's apartment the night before. Seemed like weeks ago to him. Everything was different.

"I'm going to check on Ben, see how he's doing," Tom said.

Becky asked, "Can you let me know? And can you tell him I'm sorry?"

"I'll tell him, if I get to talk to him," Tom said.

Tom stepped out and climbed the stairs. The super had just finished placing plywood over Tom's window and was moving down to the Lennox apartment.

Tom knocked at Ben's door. "You in there, Ben?"

Nothing.

"It's me, Tom. I'm alone. Open up," Tom said.

The door opened a crack. Tom pushed it and saw Ben walking away from him and falling onto the couch. No one had vacuumed in here. There was glass everywhere. Tom could see bits of glass on the couch, and spots of blood.

"Ben, get up, you're getting cut," Tom said. Ben didn't move. Tom went over and pulled him to his feet. Ben's jeans had older blood spots, and fresh ones. Tom walked him into the bathroom.

"Take those off," Tom said.

Ben removed his pants. He had fresh blood on his underwear as well.

"Listen, man, you have bits of glass in your clothes. You strip, take a shower. I need to shitcan your clothes. I'll vacuum the living room. Get yourself cleaned up. If you have a cut that won't stop bleeding, we'll check to make sure you don't have a sliver of glass in there."

Ben didn't say anything. Instead, he stripped naked and stepped into the shower. Tom carefully picked up Ben's clothes and brought them out to the living room. He searched a couple closets until he found a vacuum cleaner and began working his way from the top of the couch to the floor, getting as many nooks and crannies as he could. The blood on the couch would have to wait.

When Ben returned to the living room, he was wearing cotton pajama pants and a U2 t-shirt.

"You OK?" Tom asked.

"No more bleeding," Ben said.

"You sure?" Tom asked.

Ben didn't answer. He lay down on the couch once more and covered his eyes with the back of his forearm.

"It sucks," Ben said.

Tom asked, "Miguel was a good guy."

"Miguel and Becky and the brothers and even Rich and everything," Ben said. "It all just sucks."

"It does all suck, but don't mix all those together," Tom said.

"It all follows, man. Like, if I hadn't been hooking up with Becky, there wouldn't have been an argument that Miguel tried to stop by jumping into the back of that fucking truck," Ben said. "And the whole thing is stupid, but tragic, and that's how it works, man, it's all connected in stupid little strings, man. Puppets. It's all sick, man."

Tom said, "It was just bad luck." Though he wasn't so sure.

"Whatever, man. It is what it is, but Miguel's gone, the Lennoxi are fucked, Rich's life as he knew it is over, Becky's calling me, and I don't know, man," Ben said.

"She's downstairs with Winnie," Tom said.

Ben sat up. "What did she say?"

"She said she's in love with you, and she is sure she's lost you.

She's crying," Tom said.

"Of course she is, man," Ben said. "But she's upset because she thinks she lost me? What about all that 'stand by your man' shit?"

"She said she should've left Rich for you. She also said to tell you that she is sorry," Tom said.

Ben stood. "Aw man, she has nothing to be sorry about. She's amazing, man. Just a creature of passion and love, you know? I'm going to go find her."

"I told you—she's at Winnie's," Tom said.

He followed Ben out the door, but then they both stopped abruptly when Ben spun around. "Hey man, you haven't seen Rich, have you?"

"I haven't seen him. I have no idea where he is," Tom said.

Ben looked upward toward Rich and Becky's apartment, as if sniffing for trouble. Without another word, he strode down the stairs to the parking lot below. Tom saw him glance over at the police tape, the space within it completely empty now, with what remained of the truck apparently towed away. Tom watched Ben disappear beneath the balcony. He then heard a knock, Becky squeal, and the door close in quick succession.

Tom heard a voice from above. It was Rich. "Harlot."

Tom wasn't sure if he should say anything.

"It's the End Times, Tom," Rich said.

"Rich, I know it must hurt," Tom said. "Will you stay here tonight?"

"Don't worry," Rich said. "Your little pothead buddy has nothing to worry about. I'm going to head out of here."

"Where will you go?" Tom asked.

"Wherever the road takes me," he said. "South, I know that much. Florida sounds good, maybe."

"And you'll live in the RV?" Tom asked.

"The damn thing is hers," Rich said. "Her family had a little money. She bought that with her inheritance."

"And it's only in her name? She didn't put your name on the title?" Tom asked.

"Didn't seem right to put my name on her inheritance," Rich said. "Probably a mistake, now that I think of it, but that whore can keep the damn thing, far as I'm concerned." Rich's voice broke a bit at this last, but then certainty seemed to return to him and he said, "But I'm keeping all of the provisions for the End Times."

"When will you go?" Tom asked.

"I'll see out to the end of the year, I guess. Put in notice," Rich said. "The apartment is in my name."

"So, you'll just hang out here until then?" Tom asked.

"Tomorrow I'm going to drive the Honda over to my brother's place in Maine, spend the day there. Try to get my head on right. Maybe be back in a couple of days. But eventually, I'm heading south," Rich said. "Brynn has the number if the cops need to reach me."

Tom didn't know what else to say. Rich seemed finished with the conversation as well. "Goodnight, Tom. I'll see you when I get back."

"Goodnight. Try to get some sleep," Tom said.

Rich closed the door.

24

Tom was making an omelet out of leftover taco fixings when he heard shouting outside. It sounded like Winnie. He turned the stove off and ran out onto the balcony. Below in the parking lot, he saw Winnie chasing Brynn around in circles. Brynn was carrying a jug of something. Winnie was shouting for Brynn to stop, Brynn was attempting to drink from the jug as she ran. The women cut back and forth across the lot.

"What the hell is going on?" Tom called down.

Winnie glanced up as she continued to chase Brynn and then shouted, "She's drinking bleach!"

Dammit. Tom ran the length of the balcony and then bounded down the stairs.

"How much has she had?" Tom asked. He joined Winnie in trying to corner Brynn.

"Not that much, I don't think," Winnie said.

Brynn stopped suddenly and the three just stared at each other.

"Brynn, I know you're upset about Mike and Miguel and everything, but just put that down and let's talk it over," Winnie said.

Brynn looked right at Tom and then suddenly began chugging the bleach from the jug. Tom could hear great swallows of the liquid going down. He took four quick steps and tackled her with all the force one would apply in a football game. The jug went flying, and bleach sprayed from her mouth. Tom felt the back of his t-shirt become suddenly wet.

When they landed on the pavement, Brynn was already crying. She then began gagging and vomiting. Tom pulled her to her side.

"Call for an ambulance," Tom said. Winnie ran inside her apartment. When she reappeared, she was dialing on her phone.

"We need to find someone who has milk," Tom said. Winnie only shrugged as she reported Brynn's latest attempt to the 911 operator. Marie poked her head out just then, and Tom called to her, "Bring some milk!"

Brynn was coughing and sputtering. She didn't resist drinking the milk and gulped it down as readily as she had the bleach.

"My throat hurts," she said.

"Keep drinking the milk, hon," Winnie said. Marie stood by, but said nothing.

The ambulance arrived and the EMTs slowly walked over.

"She drink the bleach?" one asked.

"About a quart or so, we think," Winnie said.

"Did she vomit?" the other EMT, the tall one, asked. There was vomit all around Brynn.

"Are you kidding?" Marie said.

"Shouldn't we get her to the hospital?" Tom asked.

"She's not really in any danger," the tall EMT said. "You did the right thing. And the throwing up helps. Maybe some damage to her throat and maybe some irritation of mucus membranes, and so on. She'll be alright."

The shorter EMT asked, "You want us to transport her?"

Tom couldn't believe how indifferent they appeared. "Don't you think you should?"

"They won't do anything for her that you haven't done here," the tall EMT said.

Tom stood up, his face hot. Winnie stepped between him and the EMTs and said, "If you think she'll be okay, we can take care of her."

"We're willing to bring her in," the shorter EMT said. He seemed concerned more with liability than with Brynn's well-being.

"Just leave her," Tom said.

"Shouldn't we ask Brynn?" Marie asked.

Brynn was coughing, but no longer vomiting. She looked up. "I don't want to go."

"Will you kill yourself tonight?" Marie asked.

"I just want to lie down," Brynn said. "My throat hurts."

"Any suggestions for her throat?" Winnie said.

"Milk," the taller one said. "And no more bleach."

"It's an injury now," the shorter EMT said. "Her throat just needs to heal from the chemical burn. If for any reason you want us to come back and pick her up, it's no problem, just call."

There was an awkward pause, a silence, which was only broken by Brynn repeatedly trying to clear her throat.

"Okay, well, if she gets any worse or isn't getting better, just call 911 and we'll be back," the shorter one said. The two EMTs turned, climbed into the ambulance, and then drove away. Neither of them had even come within arm's reach of Brynn, and then they were gone.

Tom looked down at Brynn. She sat still on the asphalt. She watched the ambulance leave, and then she began to cry. Her weeping turned into a howl of pain, and she fell over once more, her shoulder landing in the vomit. Marie and Winnie stepped forward and helped Brynn to her feet. With a woman on either side of her, they walked her toward Marie's apartment.

"Will she stay with you tonight?" Tom asked.

Marie nodded, but said nothing. Winnie saw Brynn and Marie into the apartment, and then turned back to Tom as the door closed.

"That was all about Mike," Winnie said. "She is sure that her *soul mate* is going to prison for life. That asshole was probably just using her, just fucking her, in between playing grab-ass with his brother and a bunch of dynamite, and now he's given her a new reason to try to kill herself."

"You heard the EMTs," Tom said. "You can't really kill yourself with bleach. At least not easily. And it's not like she hid in her room washing down her meds with it. She was out in the parking lot."

"It's still a sign that she's fucked up," Winnie said. "And it's because of Mike."

Tom asked, "Did she come to your door?"

"I heard her crying, and when I opened the door, she was standing there with bleach," Winnie said.

Tom could feel some discomfort on his back now, not just wet but a slight burning. He couldn't imagine that going down his throat. "I've got to change and shower. Can you check on her? I will later, as well."

25

Tom sat in the living room and opened "Tupac Was the Buddha" to a random page. He read:

The Millennials continue to call themselves digital natives, as if Generation X chiseled out our thoughts on stone tablets as we sat in awe of their facility with technology. However, virtually all of the technology the Millennials use was either invented by Generation X, or was developed by Millennials standing on our digital shoulders.

They act like we are interlopers in their digital landscape, but we are the farmers to their eaters. At the risk of sounding Al-Gorian, we invented the fucking Internet, the PlayStation, the laptop, the smart phone, the iPod, and more. We designed the "cars," we built them, we built the "highways," we taught the kids to drive, and then they let us know that they were the experts.

I once tried to work on a Mac. These Millennials seem to like Macs. I hated it. For so many reasons. That metaphorical car we built? A Mac is like having a car with the hood welded shut. I wondered why they liked them, and then I realized it's because they live at the user level. They are all about living at the application level, in the world of apps. They give no thought to the man behind the curtain. They don't want that level of interaction. They don't want to know what he's doing. They don't want to know he's there. Their collective faces drop when we mention him, and they respond with a collective, "Whatever."

Like everything else in life, they like it orderly and predictable and simple. They seem to abhor the chaos that Generation X loves to bathe in, and work with. We want to make sense of things, and they want things to make sense. It's good the generations were born in the order they were.

Tom chuckled and closed the manuscript. He wished he could ask Miguel who the author was.

26

Rich did not come back as quickly as he said he might. Tom wondered if Rich would just stay away.

Tom knocked-and-opened Ben's door and stepped in. He found Becky sitting on the couch in a large t-shirt, smoking weed from a pipe. Ben came into the room and smiled. He was wearing nothing more than a t-shirt as well, but unlike Becky, his genitals were not covered by the garment. Becky exhaled and added to the growing cloud.

"What's up, man?" Ben asked.

"Not much. Just wondering if you'd heard about the trial," Tom said.

"Date is set, huh?" Ben asked.

"Just after the New Year," Tom said.

Becky flicked the lighter a few times before getting a flame and taking another long drag on the pipe.

Ben giggled. "Go easy on that shit, baby," Ben said.

Becky held her smoke.

"You going to go?" Tom asked.

"To court? Shit, no," Ben said. "Those places freak me out. I mean, I know I should support the boys and all, but, like, they had a hobby built on violence. Like, they didn't mean to hurt anyone, but explosives aren't *explosives* until they blow up, man, just noisemakers until they blow something—or some*one*—up, so yeah, I'm not into it. I'm not into going to court and listening to them try to justify playing with violent shit that has existential issues until it kills someone, and really, they will just be groveling and hoping that people let them go. Local jury of the least informed, too. No, man, not going."

Tom asked, "What if you're called as a witness? Both sides are interviewing."

"Already been interviewed," Ben said. "Don't give a shit. We're leaving, man."

"Leaving?"

Becky exhaled loudly, and then said, "In the RV."

"Going to Big Sur," Ben said.

"California?" Tom asked.

"Like Kerouac," Becky said.

Tom was a bit surprised that Becky would be familiar with Kerouac. Before the explosion, the only writing he'd heard her cite was the gospel of whomever.

"Are you serious?" Tom asked.

"We're going. We have to get away from here. The vibe is terrible, man. Like Brynn and Mike, that mess. And Miguel, of course, he was a positive life force, and that light is gone, man. And Marie is a shut-in now," Ben said.

"And even with Rich gone, Rich is everywhere," Becky said. "You know?"

"Even Winnie, man," Ben said. "What's up with her?"

Tom hadn't seen much of Winnie. "Actually, I'm having dinner with her tonight. Her place."

"Rumor is, she's leaving," Becky said.

"Baby, let her tell him," Ben said.

"Leaving?" Tom asked. They'd been together a couple times

since the cookout, and things had been strained, but Tom thought it was the tragedy. He didn't know she was leaving. Things had stayed pretty casual. They had a "thing," Winnie had called it. Fun, company, sex, food, movies. However, with the news that Winnie might be leaving, Tom felt a real pang of sadness out of proportion with their seemingly casual relationship. Clearly, she meant more to him than he had realized.

"Rumor is," Becky said.

Tom paused. Maybe she was wrong.

Ben, wanting to break the tension and silence, said, "We'll be leaving this weekend."

Tom stared for a moment before asking, "Do you have money?"

"I have money," Becky said.

Ben asked, "How about you, man? How will you pay the rent?"

Tom said, "I'm living on savings right now, and soon—unemployment checks."

"They are looking for someone at McDonald's, man," Ben said.

Tom smiled. "I'll think about it."

* * *

That evening, Tom arrived at Winnie's, and he knocked and actually waited until she opened the door. She was wearing a simple skirt with a camisole. Barefoot. Tom entered and slipped out of his own shoes. The apartment smelled like curry.

"Are you hungry?" Winnie asked.

"Are you moving away?" Tom asked.

Winnie's smile fell. "You heard?"

"I heard."

"I only told one person. I guess I told the *wrong* person," Winnie said. "I'm sorry you didn't hear it from me."

"Where are you going?" Tom asked. He stepped close, and put his hands on her shoulders.

"I'm transferring, to Syracuse University," Winnie said. "Winter break is coming up. I'll finish this semester and then start the January semester at Syracuse."

"We didn't talk about it at all," Tom said.

"Are we that serious, Tom?" Winnie asked.

"I might have wanted to come along," Tom said.

"I need to go alone," Winnie said. "To clear my head, to start new. Later, I was going to figure out who and what I wanted to bring from this life into my new life."

"And if I sit around and wait and remain available, you might decide to invite me to Syracuse? If I make the cut?" Tom asked.

"This doesn't have to be ugly," Winnie said. "We've had fun. I just need to leave."

"Everyone is leaving," Tom said.

"Everyone?"

"Well, Mike and Matt are gone. Of course, Miguel. Rich is gone. And now Becky and Ben are leaving," Tom said.

"They're leaving?"

"Funny, she knew you were leaving, but you didn't know they were," Tom said.

"Where are they going?" she asked.

"California."

"In the RV?" Winnie asked.

"On the road," Tom said. "When will you leave?"

"Before the solstice," Winnie said, and then added, "Before Christmas."

There was a moment of silence before they embraced.

"I'm sorry you found out from Becky instead of from me," she said.

Tom wanted to wish her luck in finding whatever she was looking for, or to say something clever that would defuse the whole thing. Instead, he asked, "What's for dinner?"

She leaned back and said, "Curry. Veggie curry."

He smiled. "Is it ready? It smells great."

"Just about," she said. She stepped away and went to the stove. "Want a beer or something?"

Tom looked around the apartment. Photos, little figurines, books everywhere. He was going to miss her.

Winnie served dinner, and they struggled to make small talk, to talk as they always had about books, movies, politics, and food. Discussing the other tenants in the building was no longer the light fun it had been. When dinner was eaten, they continued to work on the wine, and they drank until they found themselves stumbling to bed.

They had made love many times before, but this time it was clumsy and sad, with tears and unsure pauses, and when it was over, they were both relieved, and they both slept.

* * *

After that night, Tom didn't see Winnie again until the weekend, when they worked together to help Ben and Becky load up the Winnebago.

"So, you know the way?" Tom asked Ben.

"No sweat, man. I drive to Buffalo, then to Cleveland, Chicago, Omaha, Salt Lake, Sacramento, bang a left towards San Fran, keep heading south through Monterey, and then I get to Big Sur, man," Ben said.

"How long will it take?" Tom asked.

"Not a minute longer than it takes," Ben said. He smiled.

Winnie smiled, too, and said, "That's the way to think."

"There's no other way," Becky said. Her dirty hair was tied back in a bandanna and her new nose ring flashed in the sunshine.

"Give me a call now and then," Tom said.

"Will do," Ben said. The two men hugged, and the women hugged, and then they clumsily traded hugging partners.

"Thank Brynn again for me for adopting the cats," Becky said.

"I will," Winnie said.

Ben and Becky climbed into the Winnebago, and as they were getting ready to head out, music began playing.

Tom asked, "What is that?"

"Neutral Milk Hotel," Winnie said, and giggled. "Like it?"

"Is that the latest and greatest?"

"Formed in the 1980s. Been a few years since their last album," she said.

The RV made its way down the street, toward downtown and the interstate highway, and then disappeared behind a red brick building that housed a real estate agency.

Tom pulled Winnie into him, hugging her sideways. They both smiled.

A van pulled up. Mr. Hitch exited from it. He wore a thick fur hat, a winter jacket that had a plaid print, and he was carrying snowshoes. The van pulled away. He walked past them, without a word, and headed for his apartment. Tom and Winnie watched him until he went in. Winnie just shook her head.

"Let's get inside, I'm cold," Tom said.

"Big baby," Winnie said.

Tom smiled. "I'll see you later."

They headed for their respective apartments.

27

He wasn't there as a reporter. Tom was in Genesee County Superior Court as a friend. He had gone to the arraignment, where Mike had pleaded "not guilty." Tom had been there at the opening statements, and throughout the expert testimony.

On the stand that morning was Matt. Matt had been escorted in by the bailiff, and even with his help, he had stumbled on the step. He sat with eyes still bandaged behind huge goggle-like nearly opaque sunglasses. The yellow and green remnants of what had been horrible bruising were still visible on Matt's face, as were angry red grooves which someday would be faded scars.

Matt was a defense witness. After Mike's attorney, Ken Coté, had walked him through the events that led up to the explosion, he asked, "And why were explosives in the back of the truck, a truck owned by you and the defendant?"

Matt cleared his throat, sat a bit straighter, and said, "Because I put explosives in the truck."

Mike's attorney then asked, "When had you and the defendant placed the explosives in the truck?"

Matt turned toward the jury that he could not see and annunciated every word while saying, "Mike knew nothing of the explosives. Every bit of the explosives were mine. The defendant, Mike, had no prior knowledge; he had no way of knowing that there were explosives in the truck."

The prosecuting attorney, the county's assistant district attorney, John Plutarch, shot to his feet. "Objection! Your honor, this is a clear discovery violation. The witness's pre-trial testimony is completely different from what we're hearing now."

Mike's defense attorney said, "Your honor, we're hearing this for the first time as well."

The judge remained calm. "Approach the bench."

Tom could not hear much, but he did catch a few snippets. The judge promised the prosecution that the jury would have before them both Matt's pre-trial and trial testimony. Tom also heard something about a Richardson hearing, but the judge waved off the suggestion of such a hearing, whatever it was. The judge then said something to the prosecutor loud enough for everyone to hear. "Counselor, you will have a chance to cross examine."

Both attorneys returned to their seats. Defense attorney Coté tried to pick up where things had left off. "So, the defendant had no way of knowing that you had placed the explosives in the truck?"

Matt said, "No. He had no way of knowing."

Coté asked, "Had you ever placed explosives in the truck before?"

Matt said, "Never."

Coté asked, "Were the explosives in plain sight in the back of the pickup?"

Matt said, "No. I had them covered in a tarp."

Coté asked, "Why wouldn't the tarp have seemed suspicious?"

Matt said, "We always have a tarp back there covering tools and such."

Coté asked, "How long were the explosives in the truck?"

Matt said, "I had placed them in there less than an hour before the explosion."

Coté said, "No further questions, your honor."

The prosecutor, Plutarch, rose and asked, "You and your brother had experimented with explosives before that day, hadn't you?"

"No," Matt said. "Mike had never known about my hobby."

"What would the other tenants of your apartment building say if I brought them down here one at a time and asked them about you and your brother and explosives?" Plutarch asked.

It was Coté who rose this time. "Objection," he said. "Please the court, how could the witness possibly guess what half a dozen tenants would say?"

Tom knew what he himself would have testified, under oath. He would've said he personally knew nothing about explosives and the Lennox brothers, and he was fairly certain that the remaining tenants would've said the same. Except for maybe Mr. Hitch. Who knows what Hitch might have said?

"Sustained."

Coté sat and Plutarch tried a different approach. "Your brother has never participated with you in blowing things up?"

Matt said, "No, he has not."

Plutarch asked, "He's never helped you prepare explosives?"

"Never."

"The jury will see the deposition you gave pre-trial, when you claimed to have no knowledge of the explosives being in the truck," Plutarch said.

Matt said, "I lied. I was scared. But now that I see you are trying to hang this on my innocent brother… well, I had to come forward with the truth. The explosives were mine, and Mike had nothing to do with it."

Plutarch paused, and then asked, "He never helped you load

explosives into your truck? Not even for the purposes of your construction work?"

Matt said, "We hang sheetrock. Not much call for explosives in hanging and mudding sheetrock."

A member of the jury chuckled. Tom surveyed the men and women in the jury box; familiar faces all. A jury of his peers. A jury of his neighbors. Locals. And Plutarch, although he lived in a house on Hawthorne Street in Portage, was decidedly "from away." To everyone in the room, perhaps even to the judge, Plutarch still smelled like Massachusetts.

Tom watched as Plutarch did his own scan of the faces in the jury, and Tom saw the resignation set in. There would be no winning now. Matt had given the jury a reason to acquit Mike. And everyone—Plutarch, Coté, the jury, the judge—knew they would.

Later, when it came Matt's turn in the defendant's seat, the acquitted Mike came through for his brother in kind. Mike confessed that the explosives had been his and that his poor, blinded brother Matt had had no knowledge of them being in the truck. Plutarch tried to admit Matt's prior testimony in Mike's trial but, of course, the testimony was not allowed. Like Mike, Matt was acquitted, leaving Plutarch with nothing else to do but to complain to the press that everyone was forgetting about justice for Miguel.

Tom believed that Miguel would have forgiven the brothers, maybe even blamed it on himself for smoking while riding a unicycle. Miguel had been that kind of guy. He was probably sitting up there, high, giggling at the Lennox brothers for sticking it to The Man. Tom was less sure if it was really okay that the brothers were free.

* * *

Mike returned to the apartment, but Matt went to Boston, undergoing intensive occupational therapy and staying near the level of medical care he needed. Tom saw Mike in the lot, barely twenty feet from where the explosion had occurred. Tom asked, "Will Matt come back to the apartment eventually?"

"Don't think he wants to," Mike said.

"Where will he go?" Tom asked.

Mike said, "I don't think it would be the same anymore. I mean, we hung sheetrock together. Now he can't. We did other things together, and now he can't, and I never will again. It's all fucked up now. And every day, I have to park and see Miguel's old apartment. That kills me."

"Will you move?" Tom asked.

"Maybe. I've been thinking about it," Mike said. "But maybe I'm supposed to come here and see Miguel's old place and feel like shit about it."

"You think?" Tom asked.

"Well, nobody gets off scot-free," Mike said.

That's for sure.

"How about Brynn?" Tom asked. "What does she think?"

Mike looked up at Brynn's apartment. "I think I'll take her out of here, if I go."

"Is she doing okay?" Tom asked.

"Throat doesn't hurt anymore. Other than that, it's hard to tell," Mike said. "But I like her, and we have fun together."

"Will you marry her?" Tom asked.

Mike smiled. "Shit no. She's crazy." He turned and walked to the stairs.

28

Tom helped Winnie pack the rest of her things in boxes, but they did not carry the boxes out. The morning that she left, she packed two bags, and Tom carried them outside for her when her friend arrived in a small orange car.

"I'm Kerry," she said.

Tom shook her hand, and nothing more was said. Tom hugged Winnie, neither of them holding on very tightly.

"I'll miss you," Winnie said.

"Me, too," Tom said.

And that was it. Bags in the car. Winnie in the car. And the car drove away.

Sometimes, people just go.

When the car was out of sight, Tom went back to working in her apartment, as he promised he would. He was returning from another trip to the dumpster when Marie called him over to her door.

"Is your cable acting funny?" she asked.

"I wasn't watching TV," Tom said.

"Come look," Marie said, waving him in.

Tom entered the apartment. Light poured in through the new front window. The room was lit up, the couch looked well-used, with a rumpled crocheted blanket. Marie stood with her remote pointed at the television. On the screen, some talking head tried to make his bones shouting over the host of some cable-news show.

"It works," Tom said.

"Wait, look at this," Marie said. She changed the channel. The screen remained black for a moment, and then simple text appeared letting her know the Hallmark Channel was not currently available.

"It's just not available at the moment. I'm sure it'll be back soon," he said.

"That's not all!" she said. She changed the channel. Much the same thing happened, but this time it was Lifetime.

"These channels are just offline right now. I'm sure they're working on it," Tom said.

"Why would only the channels I like to watch be out?" she asked.

"I don't know," Tom said.

"I do. They know what I watch. They're just messing with me," Marie said.

"You're not serious," he said.

"You don't think they can figure out what I watch?" she asked.

"I'm sure they could," Tom said. "But why would they?"

"To mess with me," she said.

"Marie, they probably have ten million subscribers," Tom said. "Why would some twenty-something come to work at one of the largest cable providers in the country and set out to mess with just you?"

"I don't know. There are people like that out there," Marie said.

"But why you?" Tom asked. "How would he even begin to learn about you in particular?"

"They have computers, you know," she said.

Tom paused. "They certainly do have computers."

"That's right. They can find anyone they want," she said.

"But why mess with your cable?" Tom asked. "Why not take ESPN away from Bill Belichick or something?"

"Rich people never get messed with. They're all in it together to mess with us nobodies," she said.

"Like a conspiracy?"

"Like ants. When kids burn ants with a magnifying glass, it's not a conspiracy. It's just cruelty," Marie said.

"So, kids burn ants in the same way that the NFL's most successful coach and the cable company mess with you?" Tom asked.

"You brought up Belichick. I didn't say he was involved," she said. "Unless you know something I don't?"

"I didn't mean to implicate anyone," Tom said. He honestly couldn't decide whether or not to pursue this further.

"I'm just saying that those pencil necks down at the cable company got nothing else going on, probably bored out of their minds, so I'm saying maybe this kid comes to work and randomly picks someone and looks up what she watches and then turns off those channels. Just to mess with people. To feel powerful, because you know they're bored down there. The cable-company leeches probably don't even let their employees watch for free at work," Marie said.

"I'm sure they don't," Tom said.

"Right, so I'm not saying it's a big deal. I'm just saying it's too much of a coincidence that I have 700 channels and two of them don't work and it's the two I watch," Marie said.

"How many did you check?" Tom asked.

"OK, Tom, don't piss me off," Marie said.

Tom couldn't help but smile. "Alright, I'm sorry."

Marie switched back and forth between the two dark channels. "Wait, I know, I'll go check my television. I never watch those two channels. If they are out in my apartment, then we know it's nothing personal," Tom said. "Right?"

She looked skeptical, but nodded in agreement. Tom left, returned to his apartment, locked the door, and went to bed. He slept the rest of the day away.

29

Tom sat at the table and opened the "Tupac" manuscript to a random page once more. He read:

As a generation, the coolest movies were aimed right at us. There were a lot of movies that we enjoyed, but the ones made for us and about us also shaped us. Movies like *The Breakfast Club*, *Footloose*, and *Top Gun*. *Dazed and Confused*, *Singles*, and *Risky Business*. *Reality Bites*, *Ferris Bueller's Day Off*, and *Clerks*. *Fight Club*, *Snatch*, and *Office Space*. *Say Anything*, *Boyz n the Hood*, and *Sixteen Candles*.

The Millennials wear the clothing we wore in 1985. They still straighten their hair though, as if living in 1970s, and they will never resurrect the mullet, except perhaps those who are especially fond of NASCAR.

Gen-X's music must have been all right, because the Millennials are listening to covers of our music, or else so-called "new music" that so resembles songs from the 1980s that it makes us wonder if we first heard it while fooling around in the backseat of a 1978 Plymouth Duster while kissing the lip gloss off the mouths of our girlfriends. I can almost smell that blend of Aqua Net and Love's Baby Soft whenever a new Arctic Monkeys tune begins to play.

I try to listen to Millennials, but there is precious little to hear beyond the clicking of their thumbs, and what they communicate to each other rarely amounts to more than "What's up?" and "Nothing much." Generation X reads and thinks and speaks and writes. Zadie Smith and David Foster Wallace and Jonathan Franzen and Nathan Englander, et al. Tupac Shakur read voraciously. He read titles that all but the most intellectually curious Millennials would avoid at all costs. Tupac read Pirsig and Orwell and Miller and Wright and Styron. He read *Ponder on This* and *The Phenomenon of Man* and *The Destiny of Nations* and *The Souls of Black Folk*. Tupac was no punk. In Tupac, one easily finds the Buddha.

I know the Buddha is within the Millennials also, but I bet the Buddha among them thinks it is so ironic and banal of us to look at all. A half-naked fat man rolling his eyes and whispering "Whatev. So lame."

30

Tom woke in the middle of the night to noises upstairs. Again, what sounded like falling, and passion. Screams. And then something new. Breaking glass. And more screaming. Were Mike and Brynn fighting? Maybe over leaving? More smashing glass. Tom got up. He pulled on a pair of pajama pants and his winter jacket. He stepped into a pair of slippers. Then came a long scream from Brynn. And running footsteps.

Tom went out and climbed the stairs. Reaching Brynn's door, he didn't knock, but entered just in time to see Rich push a chair out of the way as he pursued Brynn across the room. Brynn screamed again. Blood was running from her left nostril and over her lip, and her torn shirt left most of her left breast exposed.

"What the hell are you doing?" Tom shouted.

Rich stopped and looked at Tom. He was enraged, and scarcely looked like the man he had been when they had first met. He turned back toward Brynn who was cowering against the kitchen counter. Rich lunged at her.

"Let her go!" Tom shouted.

Rich had her by the wrists and she was kicking at his legs, trying to score a groin hit. She was shrieking and crying.

Tom charged forward and wrapped his arm around Rich's neck and tried to pull him off in a headlock.

Rich shouted, "Becky got to fuck her hippie, I want to get mine!"

"Get off me, you pig!" Brynn screamed.

Tom gave a hard yank and twist, and Rich released Brynn. Rich turned, rotating inside Tom's arm, and delivered two hard punches to Tom's gut. Tom couldn't hold on. Rich grabbed him by the throat, both men went to the floor. Tom felt Rich's hands close around his throat as the bigger man began to choke him.

Tom couldn't breathe. He saw stars. He punched at Rich with everything he had left. It wasn't enough. Tom was sure that the last thing he'd ever see was Rich's crazed face... and then just his mouth... and then just one drop of spittle hanging from the lower lip... but then Rich's grip loosened and the man fell away.

The air rushed into Tom's lungs. In his vision, the room gained light and color. Tom couldn't stop gagging. He could taste copper in each cough.

He rose to his hands and knees. Brynn ran into the other room, still screaming, and slammed the door behind her. Tom looked at Rich, who was lying on the floor beside him, face down, with a knife handle sticking out of his shoulder.

Rich said, "She killed me. The little bitch killed me."

Tom moved to Rich's side. The wound was too high for vital organs, but he could still bleed out.

"Brynn! Call 911!" Tom said.

"Fuck you!" Brynn called from her bedroom.

"Brynn! Just call!" Tom said. He applied pressure to the wound.

"Take the knife out," Rich said. He moaned and rocked a bit under Tom's hands.

"I can't. It could cut something on the way out too, plus it might be plugging up a hole it already cut. We have to leave it, and let a surgeon remove it," Tom said.

Rich moaned again. "Tom? Who am I? Who am I now?"

Tom said, "Just take it easy, Rich."

"Who am I? Do you know? Do you know who you are? Who are we?" Rich asked.

"Brynn!" Tom shouted.

"They're coming!" she shouted back.

* * *

After the ambulance and police arrived, Rich was taken out on a gurney before Tom and Brynn could finish explaining what had happened. Once they had explained, the police radioed that the only person under arrest was Rich. Brynn was to come down to the station the next day and speak to a detective, but she appeared to be in the clear.

An EMT returned to the apartment. "Do you need to go to the hospital, Brynn?" He was the older of the two EMTs who had responded when Brynn had leapt from the balcony.

Brynn was wrapped in a blanket taken from the couch. Her nosebleed had stopped and was cleaned up. She shook her head.

Mike suddenly appeared in the doorway. "Brynn?"

"She's okay," Tom said.

Mike came in and held her, and she began crying again. The EMT left with half a wave.

"I thought maybe I'd lost you this time," Mike said. "Why were they loading Rich into the ambulance?"

"I stabbed him!" Brynn said.

"What for?" Mike asked.

"He was crazy! He attacked me! Said he wanted to fuck me 'cuz of Becky and Ben," she said.

"He said what?" Mike asked. His face went to a dark shade of red.

"Tom saved me," Brynn said, still crying.

Mike looked up. Tom said nothing.

"Thank you," Mike said.

Tom said, "She saved me right back, that's how Rich got stabbed. He was strangling me, and Brynn stabbed him to get him to stop."

Mike smiled into Brynn's face. "You're pretty tough, you know that?" Tom thought Mike was trying to cheer Brynn, but Mike himself looked more than a little unhinged, with the fake smile and the virtual high-five over stabbing a man. Brynn did laugh, between sobs and great sniffles of snot.

Tom was tired and his throat was still sore. "Are you two going to be okay?"

Brynn said, "We're okay. Thanks again."

"We're okay," Mike said.

Tom said, "Alright, goodnight." He stepped out onto the balcony in time to see the last police cruiser pull away.

31

A very low chain-link fence surrounded the cemetery out on Fairgounds Road. There was an archway, suspended on two black posts, which served as an entrance. In wrought iron, the words "Riverview Cemetery" were spelled out. It was closed for the season, and there were patches of early snow.

Tom parked next to the fence and walked in. He carried a backpack on one shoulder, and headed for the far left end of the cemetery. There, just short of the narrow circuitous dirt road, was Miguel's fresh grave. Tom was grateful that they were able to get him in before the ground froze. Frankly, he was surprised that Miguel had not been cremated. Being buried and occupying green space for all eternity, or at least the next few hundred years, didn't seem Miguel's style, but his family had insisted that he be buried right there in Portage.

Tom pulled a thick circular pad, like a nylon pillow, from the pack. This he set on the ground next to the fresh-turned earth that lay atop Miguel's casket. He sat crossed-legged on the pad, and placed the pack at his feet. He drew the bong from the pack and placed this between his body and the bag. It was somewhat shielded from the casual observer, but anyone who cared to look would have seen it. Tom didn't care.

He packed the bowl, applied the flame, pulled smoke into the chamber, and then released it into his lungs. He felt the soothing effects almost immediately. He took another hit.

He looked at the simple stone. Grey, deeply etched, traced with black within each letter. Miguel Lacosta had lived only forty years. No epitaph, except for two words, "Happy child." Tom wondered if the intent had been accusatory, as if as a child his family had thought Miguel was happy and perfect and normal before everything went "wrong." He preferred to think that they had captured the essence of Miguel as an adult, forever the happy child, despite the psychic load he was carrying.

Miguel had died in an effort to make peace. That, coupled with his suffering and childlike love, must have ensured him a place in...what? Heaven?

He took another bong hit. A man on a bicycle went by, but he didn't notice Tom.

"Who are you?" Rich had asked. Tom didn't know anymore. He had been a mildly ambitious and certainly cynical reporter when he had arrived in Portage, writing a novel, with dreams of that lucrative book deal. Now he was unemployed and smoking weed beside the fresh grave of a man he had hardly known.

What was his purpose now? To chase dreams? He no longer had any, and it was liberating. No longer was there a yardstick against which to measure success and failure. To have a wife and kids? Even if that gave purpose to a life, raising one's children was over about halfway through life, notwithstanding the sentiment that "they'll always need you," which Tom didn't really believe. To simply work to acquire knowledge? To what end? So that he could be a Russian-speaking pothead-philosopher serving fries to drunken teenagers at 11pm on a Friday night?

To serve God, to be saved, and enjoy eternal reward? It was the safe bet, even if it turned out there wasn't a God, but it seemed if you tried too hard, the Devil took precise aim at you and fucked up your life anyway. To be sincere, to spread love and peace? You could be blown up in the effort and still not leave peace behind in your wake. Perhaps he should simply put his head down, forget about a career, and just find a job, and find joy in the distractions. But how much would be enough distraction? Would he find himself playing with explosives? Maybe he should believe in the demon-haunted world, or universe, and accept that things can't be as simple and bleak as they appear. That there must be a plan, and we're just too insignificant to understand it. That someday the architects will return and reveal all. Perhaps feeling you were one of the few who knew the "truth" provided enough of a sense of power to mitigate the feelings of helplessness.

Maybe seeking beauty in all things and causing no intentional injury to sentient beings was enough, so that even if one did no good, at least one did no harm. Still, it seemed to Tom that even vegans eat people.

Tom took another bong hit and blew the smoke at Miguel's grave.

"What do you think, Miguel?" Tom asked. "What's next?"

Tom looked at the bong, and then at the grave. A squirrel chattered loudly in the nearby treetops. The grass was cold, almost crunchy. Tom looked at the bong and grave again. There were no answers here.

He tapped out the bowl on the ground, and did not return it to its seat in the bong. He stood, poured the bong water over the grave, and then leaned the bong itself against the stone. Tom tried to throw the bowl into the tree line, but instead it fell among the graves of the young children, their diminutive white headstones clumped together like the kindergarten class they never saw.

Tom said, "Take it easy, bro. Rest easy."

Tom turned and walked away. He would never return. He would go look for answers from a different source.

* * *

He drove back to the apartments and found his sister, Trisha, waiting for him on the stairs. She stood as he parked, but did not approach his car.

"I didn't know you were coming," Tom said, and immediately regretted that his tone wasn't warmer.

"It was pretty spontaneous," Trisha said.

Tom hugged her as he arrived on the steps. "Let's go up."

She followed without a word. Once they were in the apartment, he walked into the kitchen. Trisha didn't follow. When he returned, she was still standing just inside the door.

"What's up?" Tom asked.

"Tom, there was an explosion here, a person was killed, and then I hear about a stabbing at this same place," Trisha said.

"Yeah, I know about those," Tom said. He moved to the couch and sat. He rubbed his forehead.

"What are you doing here?" Trisha said. She approached and sat on the coffee table.

"It's where I live," Tom said.

"But why do you live here?" she asked. "You could find something else."

"I know you're worried, but I wish you would've called before you drove all this way. I'm okay. I'm home here," Tom said.

"That doesn't make me worry less," Trisha said.

"These people, they have their quirks, but they're genuine people. They are not caught up in the rat race. They've stepped outside the 'social OK' and so they are refugees here. I live in a refugee camp, but I've come to like it. I know I like me better when I'm with them, as opposed to having to listen and submit to some idiotic and patronizing boss," Tom said.

"But people have *died*," Trisha said.

"I was there," Tom said. "And the stabbing, too. But I'm not leaving here."

Trish stood up. "Are you losing it?"

"Losing what?" Tom asked. "My dreams of being the best refrigerator news writer I can be?"

"Just come stay with me for a while. You can get away from this and get back on track," Trish said.

"I don't want to be on that track anymore. Call it a mid-life crisis or a delayed adolescence, whatever, but I'm going to see where this path takes me," Tom said.

"Winnie had the sense to leave," Trish said. "Why not go with her?"

"She didn't invite me," Tom said. "No, I'm staying. I'm too curious not to stay. I want to see where I end up when I'm not letting someone else steer."

"Are you steering?" Trish asked.

"Don't worry," Tom said. He rose and they embraced.

"I'll always worry," Trish said.

"I wish you wouldn't," Tom said. "Want to spend the night?"

"I can't," Trish said.

"How about staying for dinner?" Tom said.

She nodded. "That'd be nice, thanks."

That afternoon and evening, they talked about Winnie, about the neighbors, and about jobs, kids, and plans. Around 9:00 p.m., Trish stood up.

"I've got a two-hour drive, I should head home," Trish said.

"Sure you wouldn't rather stay?" Tom asked.

"I'd like to, but not tonight," she said.

Tom walked her to the door and down to her car. Once seated in it, she rolled the window down.

"I'll be fine," Tom said.

"Call me," Trish said.

32

Tom woke to a light flooding into his bedroom simultaneously from the window and the hallway. He reflexively glanced at the clock; it was 3:00 a.m. He jumped out of bed and, screening his eyes with his outstretched hand, made his way to the window. He could see nothing but white light. There was a slight vibration in the floor, but no sound.

And then he was in his living room. And the clock on the cable box read 4:20 a.m. *What the hell?* He slowly walked out onto the balcony. Mike was to his left. His hands were on the railing. Tom moved to the railing, and placed his hands on it. Mr. Hitch appeared below.

"Marie is gone, boys," Hitch said. He then disappeared beneath the balcony once more, directly below where Tom was standing. Mike and Tom made their way down the stairs, and then to Marie's apartment. They reached the open door just as Hitch was coming out. He handed a piece of paper to Tom.

It read:

"I wish you all well. He allowed me to leave you this note. He's human, beautiful, and he looks half-black and half-white. You know, like coffee? I forget what that's called. Not the coffee—the people that are half-and-half. Well, whatever. I asked where he was from and he said New Hampshire, but that he grew up with them. Don't that beat all? He says there are others. I'm going with them. Why they want an old hag like me, I don't know, but I'm happy. Don't worry about me. Oh, he says you can write me. Just leave letters in a coffee can or something in the bushes at the base of the sign at the Whale's Tale Waterpark, just south of Indian Head, out on Rt. 3. You'll find it. When I can, I'll write back. Tell Tom we don't need this in the paper. And tell Hitch he was right. —Marie Dupuis"

Tom looked up. Hitch was walking away.

"What were you right about?" Tom asked.

Hitch didn't respond. Mike took the note and read it. "No fuckin' way," he said.

Tom watched Hitch climb the stairs. It was time to have a talk with Hitch, he decided.

33

The next day, Tom sat to write a letter of his own. He began:

"Dear Winnie,

Marie is gone. It seems aliens came by and picked her up. She left a very nice note. Other than that, and Rich attacking Brynn, and Brynn stabbing him (but not fatally), not much has happened since you left.

I went to see Miguel the other day. We smoked a bit and talked a bit. I did most of the talking. He sends his best."

Tom sat back and thought for a moment. What was all this? What the hell was he writing? He continued:

"Okay, I'm an asshole. Everything I wrote above is true, but I was still trying to sound cool writing it. I'm an asshole because I have adopted the same defensive force-field so many people our age, or maybe more accurately, my age use. We work hard to appear to not care about anything, because whatever we care about can be used to mock us, or even hurt us. We wear the Teflon-coated suit of nihilism, we say snarky shit whenever we might appear sincere and thus vulnerable, and we never say, directly, what we mean. We deflect, we dissemble, we distance.

I want to be real. I want to be sincere and optimistic. I want irony to be gone, and I want to trust again. I want to be energized, instead of either being tired or acting tired.

And in the short time that I've been in Portage, I've seen glimpses of the bright sunshine of hope, of signs of life with feelings, and of peace and love.

I felt it most of all with you. There, I said it. Unoriginal, without irony, naïve and sentimental. Maybe I'm being over-credulous. Maybe I want to stay that way. I miss you, Winnie, and I love you."

He reread it, signed it, and folded it. He walked into the kitchen, pulled an envelope down from a cupboard, and stuffed the letter inside. He retrieved Winnie's new address and copied it to the envelope.

The next day, he mailed it.

34

Tom knocked on the door at apartment 3C. He waited. The door opened. Mr. Hitch stood there in a Hawaiian shirt, jeans, and Adidas man-dals.

"Can I come in?" Tom asked.

Mr. Hitch backed away, and Tom stepped past him. The apartment had no single theme, but was decorated with items from every corner of the world. On a single shelf, Tom saw a piece of pottery that was probably Peruvian, a wooden carving that looked Polynesian, and a doll that was clearly Japanese. Above these hung an impressionist painting, in bright golds and reds, of Masai warriors. Tom recognized the music as an Indian pop song, a Bollywood thing, called "Chaiya Chaiya" or something like that. The room smelled not of marijuana, but of patchouli.

Hitch closed the door and followed him in. "Have a seat, Tom."

Tom picked a spot on the couch. He sat and Hitch sat immediately beside him, in his personal space. Tom stood.

"Go ahead and sit, Tom," Hitch said. He patted the couch where Tom had just been. Tom slowly sat. The two men were looking at each other and, despite being so close, they were not touching.

"Have you come to interview me?" Hitch asked.

"I don't work for the paper anymore," Tom said.

"That's not what I asked," Hitch said.

Tom thought for a moment. "I suppose I have."

"Ask away," Hitch said.

Tom was still rigid; he had his hands on his own knees, sitting awkwardly straight. Hitch's face was perhaps a foot from Tom's. What could he ask?

"What do you think really happened to Marie?" Tom asked. "What did she mean, you were right? Right about what?"

"Not a very good starting point," Hitch said.

Tom bristled. This was awkward enough.

"What *would* be a good starting point?" Tom asked.

"What's the last thing you would ask me? Let's start at the end," Hitch said.

"Are you gay?" Tom asked.

"Sometimes," Hitch said. "Why would that be the last thing you'd ask?"

Tom said, "Because it is none of my business."

"Identifying ourselves in relation to others is everyone's business," Hitch said.

"Well, I know I'm not gay," Tom said.

Hitch shrugged. "Nobody's perfect."

Tom studied him a bit. He moved his face closer to Hitch's. If he were gay, Hitch would certainly not be his type. The man was older, overweight, with tired eyes, and a receding hairline.

"I won't kiss you," Hitch said.

"What?" Tom said.

"I'm not into you. You're leaning closer, thinking about what it would be like to kiss. But I won't kiss you," Hitch said.

"I thought you were only gay sometimes," Tom said.

"Right, so I won't kiss you," Hitch said.

What the hell was happening?

"Who are you?" Tom asked.

"Ah, the first question," Hitch said. He leaned back a bit. "I am Alphonse Hitch. Adventurer."

"Living in Portage," Tom said.

"You think that's boring?" Hitch asked.

Tom thought for a moment. Brynn's leap. Becky and Ben. Winnie. The Lennoxes, Miguel's death, Rich stabbed. Marie. And *this* guy.

"It's not boring," Tom said.

"You timed your arrival perfectly," Hitch said.

"I thought maybe I'd caused it all," Tom said.

"Whew, what an ego," Hitch said. "Now I know I don't want to sleep with you."

"I'm not gay," Tom said.

"Stop apologizing," Hitch said.

What? "I mean, I thought I had upset the karmic balance or whatever."

"I know what you meant," Hitch said. "You overestimate your karmic weight. It was going to go this way."

"Why am I here?" Tom asked.

"What do you want to hear?" Hitch asked. "I mean, I could try to sound like a fortune cookie if you'd like."

Tom said, "There must be some reason for it all. For Miguel dying, for Rich and Becky's lives imploding, for Brynn, for Mike and Matt, for Marie... There must be some reason."

"Why?" Hitch asked.

"Doesn't it all have to *be* for something? Part of a larger plan?"

"Why?" Hitch asked again. "So all this shit can be less scary?"

"If for no other reason, then, yes," Tom said.

"What if there *is* no plan? What if there were no reasons? What if physics and philosophy and psychology and religion are all just bullshit, and the whole absoluteness was just random, illogical, chaotic disarray from which we desperately search to construct artificial and contrived patterns just to soothe ourselves?" Hitch asked.

Tom shook his head. "There are actual patterns. There are *real* reasons. There *is* cause and effect. Miguel is dead and there are people to blame. Rich and Becky's marriage ended because of an affair. Matt is blind because of decisions people made. Life is busy and sometimes intense, but it is *not* random."

"You want to believe that because you want to believe we have control over some part of this," Hitch said. "Ask yourself how often in the course of a day that you're surprised by something. Then, ask yourself how often you explain it away by claiming it was bad luck or coincidence. We're the only animals that acknowledge coincidence. Other animals take everything at face value. We have to edit our reality and label something that doesn't fit 'a coincidence,' so that we can dismiss it, or when that won't suffice, we call it an act of God."

"You're saying it's all totally random?" asked Tom.

"You're saying Miguel's death wasn't random, it was just bad luck. Think, Tom," Hitch said.

"What?"

"What is luck?" Hitch asked.

"Luck is… luck. You know," Tom said.

"Well, that was lucid," Hitch said.

"What is luck then?"

Hitch went to a bookshelf and pulled out a dictionary. He opened it, and then read that luck is "a purposeless, unpredictable, and uncontrollable force that shapes events favorably or unfavorably for an individual, group, or cause."

"It says that?" Tom asked.

"It reads that," Hitch said. "How is that not just a fancy way of saying the whole thing is just totally random?"

"But it's a *force*," Tom said.

Hitch said, "A force that is purposeless serves nothing. A force that is unpredictable follows no pattern. A force that is uncontrollable would be better ignored."

Tom paused, but then he reasserted himself. "We are not talking about abstractions. Real people are dead and hurt, lives are changed and ruined."

"So, what are you going to do next?" Hitch asked.

Tom had no idea. "What did Marie mean when she said you were right?"

"She didn't say it, she wrote it," Hitch said.

"Okay, when she wrote that you were right."

Hitch said, "I told her that they would come for her."

"You really think spacemen took her?" Tom asked.

"How would you explain it?" Hitch asked.

Tom paused for a moment. "Why would they come here?"

"They've been taking people for a long time from here. They've got sort of a little terrarium here, I think, between the lakes and the notch," Hitch said.

Tom didn't say anything. At this point, Tom didn't know what to believe and what not to believe.

"What's the next step?" Hitch asked.

Tom wasn't sure. He stood and walked across the room. "I just want it to mean something."

"What? What do you want to mean something?"

"I want Miguel to have more of a legacy than a stone no one will visit," Tom said.

"You want *you* to have more of a legacy than a stone," Hitch said.

"Alright, fine, *all* of us. I want all of us to mean a bit more than what our daily existence represents," Tom said.

Hitch said, "Write a book."

"I started one, but it was all horseshit," Tom said.

Hitch said, "Write a book about your time in Portage. Extend the story by getting it down on paper. Extend all of us."

"No one will believe it," Tom said.

Hitch chuckled. "Tell them it's fiction. Some of them will believe it then. Insist that it's purely fiction, and everyone will believe it really happened."

"Fictionalize it?"

"Just enough so people think it's true," Hitch said.

"Like change the names?" Tom said.

"Sure. And the town. Have it take place in something like 'Plymouth' instead of Portage," Hitch said.

Tom smiled. "Plymouth, New Hampshire? Won't people think of the pilgrims?"

"All the more reason," Hitch said.

With each passing moment, the idea became more and more attractive. "Who the hell would read a book about aliens, drywall, and a unicycle?"

Hitch grinned, "There are a lot of nuts out there."

Tom smiled. "What do I do for money while I write this book?"

"As little as possible," Hitch said.

"Sounds pretty good," Tom said. "Why don't *you* write a book?"

"I did," said Hitch. He reached again into the bookshelves, and pulled out a box. He opened it, and handed a manuscript to Tom. The title read, "Tupac Was the Buddha."

"You wrote this?" Tom said. "I've been reading it!"

"How did you get it?"

"Miguel lent me a copy," Tom said.

"So that's where that copy went," Hitch said. "So, what did you think of it so far?"

Tom said, "It's good, but so far, it sounds mostly like throat clearing. I thought there was a lot more to be written. I know I wanted to read more."

Hitch asked, "It began to feel like a rant. I'm not sure I have that much more to rant about."

Tom said, "Keep writing your observations. Our generation needs a touchstone book."

Hitch looked at the manuscript. He flipped a few pages. "But this isn't the book that will extend our individual stories; these are just the musings of a weirdo. You're the one who will extend us. Write about us here in the Cooper building and Portage."

"I'm not sure I'm the right guy to write that, or that I even deserve to," Tom said.

"I think you're perfect for the job. You came from the outside, you came in judgmental and with a feeling of superiority, but then you became sympathetic, you fell in love with one of us, and you came to *see* the rest of us," Hitch said.

"Us?" Tom asked. "You consider yourself one of them?"

"Why shouldn't I?"

"You're always so aloof," Tom said. "None of them know anything about you."

"I'm shy."

Tom paused, and then said, "You seem like a nice guy. You're worldly, and well-read, and you'd have a lot to offer the tenants."

"So?"

"So why don't you?" Tom asked. "Why don't you engage and advise?"

"That would be awfully egotistical of me. It's not like my life is a model for others."

"And the book, you could write another book," Tom said. "I mean, extending the story of these people wouldn't have to be up to me. You have enough perspective to write that book."

"I've been here too long. We've both gone native, but you still remember the homeland. Write the book with perspective and love, Tom," Hitch said.

Tom said, "You are really weird, you know."

Hitch walked straight at Tom, and kissed him. Tom didn't pull away. He felt Hitch's tongue briefly brush his own, his mouth tasted slightly of licorice, and then Hitch pulled back and stepped away.

Hitch said, "You're not gay."

Tom shook his head. "I knew that."

"We're both sure now," Hitch said.

"Thanks," Tom said.

"Just write the book, Tom," Hitch said.

Tom wiped his mouth. Hitch adjusted his shirt and headed for the kitchen. Tom waited a minute, but Hitch said nothing more. Tom could hear him loading the dishwasher.

"I'll show myself out," Tom said softly. He opened the door and stepped out into the winter air, and pulled it closed behind him. He walked past first Brynn's apartment and then Rich-and-Becky's old place before turning down the stairs. He passed Ben's vacant apartment, and entered his own. So, a book. A new project.

He licked his lips. Licorice. He shook his head.

35

Tom started the tape recorder. Mike and Brynn sat back on her couch. The D.A. was reportedly mulling over bringing new charges against the brothers, but the inside scoop was they weren't sure they could make anything stick in light of the brothers' defense scheme. Because they had been found not guilty, and their rent had never been late, the brothers were not even evicted.

The sunlight was warm, and reflecting off the yellow walls.

"Brynn, let's pick up where we left off yesterday," Tom said.

Brynn nodded, and Mike took her hand.

"You haven't been 'in crisis' in some time," Tom said.

Brynn licked her lips.

"Right?" Tom asked. Lip-licking wouldn't record well.

Brynn cleared her throat. "Right."

"What's changed?" Tom asked. "Was it Miguel? Did that make you reassess your contribution to the world, or your place in life?"

"Oh my God, that's *so* cliché," Brynn said.

"Yeah, that really sucks, dude," Mike said. Mike shifted in his seat.

"What then? Finding love?" Tom said.

Brynn groaned.

"This book is going to suck," Mike said.

Tom leaned back in the chair. He looked at the fish.

"It was you," Brynn said.

"Me?" Tom said.

"You were working for The Man, all important, writing the news and all that, but in the end, you haven't accomplished anything either. You couldn't save anyone, not even yourself," Brynn said.

Tom didn't like where this was going. "How did that help you?"

"I was feeling insignificant. Turns out, we all are. I mean, in the big scheme of things. None of us really matter. Once I got that, I realized I wasn't missing out on anything," Brynn said.

"Actually, I'm writing the book to extend our presence," Tom said. *Extend the story*, Hitch had said, but Tom liked the idea of extending their presence.

Mike laughed. "You go ahead and do that, man."

Brynn said, "I get it, but just because someone hangs around longer than someone else, either alive or as a memory, doesn't make them more important. Mike's got stuff in his fridge from last summer. Doesn't make it more important than the other stuff in there. But the fridge 'extended' it."

"Leave them olives alone, honey," Mike said. They both giggled.

Tom winced.

The interview continued, without much more of interest or value, and after an hour or so, Tom packed up his recorder and left. As he came down the stairs, he saw a small car pull in. The passenger door opened, and out stepped Winnie. She went to the backseat and pulled a couple bags to the ground. She thanked the driver, closed the door, and the little car drove away. Tom watched her from the second floor balcony until she noticed him.

"Hey you," Winnie said.

"Hey," Tom said. "Are you back?"

"I got your letter," Winnie said, smiling. "I changed my mind.

I think I'll stick around here a while, at least until the January semester begins."

"Your old apartment is still available, I think. No one has moved in yet," Tom said.

"I'm only here a few weeks. Can't I stay with you?" she asked.

Tom smiled and made his way down the stairs, "Can I crash for a couple years in Syracuse?"

Winnie grinned. "I've got just the couch."

Tom laughed, and said, "Let me take you out to dinner. We can celebrate."

Winnie asked, "Celebrate my flakiness?"

"Whatever you say," Tom said. "How about a steak house?"

"I won't go out with you, but I'll cook for you here," she said.

"You will?" Tom asked.

"Your place, around dinner time," she said.

"What time is that?"

"Around 9:00 p.m."

"You eat late," Tom said, finally reaching her, and brushing some hair from her face.

"Everyone else eats too early," she said, and wrapped her arms around his neck.

"Around 9:00 p.m. then," Tom said, holding her. "Can I go get anything for dinner?"

Winnie smiled and said, "Please don't."

They kissed. He had missed her.

Acknowledgments

Erik Johannes, who read the first drafts of this novel, and was always intensely encouraging. Because I couldn't tell if he was being sarcastic or not, I kept writing it.

Robert Pirsig (whom Winnie paraphrases on the hike), for the hours and hours of time spent reading and contemplating *Zen and the Art of Motorcycle Maintenance* and *Lila*. Thank you.

To Nylah Lyman for the support and encouragement to keep writing through the years, despite and because of all the ups and downs.

To Olivia Bradley and Lauren Stetson, for reading and providing great feedback. I always looked forward to hearing what you thought of the work-in-progress.

To Marta Nesbitt, who encouraged me to return to the manuscript, after my not touching it for sometime, with advice on how to improve it. She was the first person to say she loved it.

To Tupac Shakur, you definitely were no punk. If only you'd lived to be an old man, with grandchildren around your feet. So much left unshared.

To the real Hitch who kept me company during a lot of the writing. There's nothing like an old border collie. RIP, buddy.

Chase Street Market in Plymouth, New Hampshire, where a bunch of this book was written in one sunny corner. It's a lovely, welcoming space. There were many days when I was there long enough to order both breakfast and lunch sandwiches, which were always delicious.

About the Author

Kevin St. Jarre is the author of *Aliens, Drywall, and a Unicycle*, his first novel with Encircle Publications. He previously penned three original thriller novels for Berkley Books, the Night Stalkers series, under a pseudonym. He's a published poet, his pedagogical essays have run in *English Journal* and thrice in *Phi Delta Kappan*, and his short fiction has appeared in journals such as *Story*. He has worked as a teacher and professor, a newspaper reporter, an international corporate consultant, and he led a combat intelligence team in the first Gulf War. Kevin is a polyglot, and he earned an MFA in Creative Writing with a concentration in Popular Fiction from University of Southern Maine's Stonecoast program. Twice awarded scholarships, he studied at the Norman Mailer Writers Center on Cape Cod, MA, with Sigrid Nunez and David Black, and wrote in southern France at La Muse Artists & Writers Retreat. He is a member of MWPA and the International Thriller Writers. Born in Pittsfield, Massachusetts, Kevin grew up in Maine's northernmost town, Madawaska. He now lives on the Maine coast, and is always working on the next novel. Follow Kevin at www.facebook.com/kstjarre and on Twitter @kstjarre.

CPSIA information can be obtained
at www.ICGtesting.com
Printed in the USA
LVHW030102141021
700343LV00003B/432

9 781645 990673